Grim Oceans, Savage Plains

An Arthur Wilson & Benjamin Hathorne Novella

by
Max Beaven

Cover design by Jeff Brown

"Vaunting aloud, but racked with deep despair."
John Milton

Table of Contents

February 1898

Prologue

Marblehead Harbor, Massachusetts

Captain Henry Watkins watched as sporadic waves hit up against the pilings. Sometimes a light salty spray would drift over the edge of the dock. The skies were dark, but thus far kept their torrents at bay. He glanced at his timepiece. It was twenty minutes to four. They'd need to set sail soon. He knew his crew was ready, they were a tight bunch. His concern was the weather. They'd only be going out so far as the islands. He had a copy of the route in his journal, drawn out on a chart by the dandy who'd hired him.

He sighed, and slowly walked towards the jolly boat that would take him out to his ship. Sailors were a superstitious lot, and if they knew the true reasons behind this voyage some might balk. He didn't understand what the young man hoped to accomplish, but the pay was too good to pass up. Aside from concerns about the looming weather, the crew should be looking forward to getting paid for what might be considered a pleasure cruise. He was told the timing was critical, and he was a man of his word, even if he thought the whole idea preposterous.

He nodded to the men to begin rowing and took a last

glance back at Blackler's salt house. There was a lot of history there, and few ships set anchor here now. Only the wealthy with their yachts up at the Corinthian——the thought caused him to spit over the side. The small boat gradually drew nearer his merchantman Whateley. He could see his crew moving with purpose around the deck. Good lads. With one or two exceptions, they'd all been with him for a number of years. That was rare. He was given to do a bit of smuggling here and there, though he also took on legitimate cargo and the periodic charter, and most would hire on a crew for the job.

His men brought the boat alongside and he moved easily up the ladder, the learned practice of many years. He looked about, and spotting his first officer on the quarterdeck, moved aft to approach him. "Are we ready Joseph?"

Joseph was looking at a chart. "We're ready. Though this may be the shortest and most pointless trip we've made, if for the most reward."

Henry smiled; Joseph was dour as ever. "All the more reason to get started."

Joseph glanced at him sideways. "We could anchor out beyond one of the islands for a few hours and he'd be none the wiser."

The captain shook his head, "You know better than that. We honor our contracts. There's no danger and it's as idle a cruise as we've made anyway."

Joseph nodded, rolling up the chart and turning to the

pilot to start giving directions. This was followed by the shouts and motion of a seasoned crew going about their tasks. The captain looked out towards the ocean, his years of experience telling him that they should have already seen rain, but the clouds seemed content to simply darken the sky. The ship began its slow progress out of the harbor. Henry looked starboard for the small skeletal lighthouse there. It was barely visible in the gloom. Small comfort, he thought.

Joseph came back, "Why do you think they passed so close to Children's Island?"

"Hard to say. They were amateur sailors, could be they simply used it as a point of reference. Regardless, that's the route we'll take." He looked out towards the barely visible mass. "Carefully."

"I'm always careful Captain." He headed over to the pilot and spoke into his ear.

Henry was watching the skies again. Still no rain, no wind. It should be pouring. His crew did an admirable job with the currents and low wind. Soon they were moving along at around eight knots.

Reaching into his overcoat, he removed his journal from an interior pocket. The edges of a few sheets of fine paper stuck out from the pages. He removed them. A planned travel route, as provided by the Hathorne couple. A map, drawn by their son Benjamin, and an accompanying document specifying dates, times, and recorded weather and tidal information for the evening they went missing. It was quite detailed, and as accurate as conjecture could provide. He did not believe they would find any sign of the lost ship, or any indication of what might have occurred to the couple. Yet he could understand a son's grief, and if he had the resources, would probably do much the same.

The skies darkened further as the sun began its slow descent. The pilot turned the ship northward to parallel Children's Island, slowing to give a wide berth to the island and the other obstacles that littered this part of the sea. The forward crew was now taking soundings. The Hathorne's ship would have had a small keel and would have been able to venture closer, though he felt they would have exercised caution, knowing a shipwreck here would lead to them seeking aid at the sanitarium.

Now in safer waters, they picked up speed slightly. Benjamin had insisted that his parents would have followed their timetable religiously. His explanation for wanting to replicate this journey, was in his words, "to recreate the voyage on the exact date and time, including the astrological alignment, to determine if there was a repeatable condition that might prevent further disasters". Henry thought the young man might have gone a bit mad. But he seemed earnest, if overly intent and he paid handsomely for any potential risk. The larger ship, with an experienced captain and crew, he believed would be able to deal with any poor weather or current anomalies that might arise.

In the tavern on the wharf, this all seemed reasonable to Henry, and they needed the work. Other than his first officer, no one knew the precise details, only that they were looking for a ship, long lost at sea, and were getting paid for their troubles regardless of outcome.

Over the last few minutes, the captain had become anxious. The sky was unusually and unnervingly dark. Some of the crew had begun to light lanterns. He glanced over at Joseph, who looked even more grim than usual; he was sensing it too. Given the direction and speed at which they were sailing, they should have spotted the Bakers Island lighthouse by now. Henry peered out into the gloom but could see neither light nor island. He turned to Joseph, who already had the crew beginning to slow, their years together making orders unnecessary in most cases. He knew what he was about.

As the manifold noises of the ship quietened, he began to hear something else. Unidentifiable at first, but as the ship cruised slowly on its northeasterly course, it seemed to be many sounds in concert. It wasn't his imagination; all about him crew members strained to hear and see where the sounds originated from.

Joseph approached, close enough to speak without being overheard by the crew. "Do you hear that?"

"Aye, I do. Is it coming from Bakers do you think?" The sounds were becoming louder, and more disturbing. Echoing bleating sounds, throaty croaking and above it all an alien singing that made the hairs on his neck stand up.

"No, the darkness is impacting navigation, but I'd say we're halfway to the island, and veered off to the northwest as planned, so that we could come around the west side of the isle and loop back around toward Salem harbor. Shouldn't be anything here. Maybe the sounds are coming from…"

His next words were cut short by a sudden impact to the ship. Henry fell hard to the port side of the quarter-deck, his head striking the bulwark and causing him to see a momentary burst of white light. He shook it off quickly, and rose, the deck now tilted downward toward the port side. They'd struck something along the starboard bow. Lanterns swung wildly, and at least one fell to the deck, engulfing part of it in flame. He opened his mouth to begin bellowing orders, when he heard the screaming.

Not the sound of men injured by falls or the other various mishaps he had heard over many years of sailing but screams of a kind he had never before encountered. Intermingling with the screams were those sounds which moments before had seemed to come from somewhere out to sea. Now they were here. On his ship.

Wet flopping, croaking, baying and bleating. A hellish discordant and appalling noise, as if the deck of his ship had been engulfed in nightmare. Past the flames, he now saw some of the things making the cacophonous sounds. He wished he hadn't. Grotesque deformities of human forms, some partially obscured by black robes, but others all too visible. Groups of them overwhelmed the members of his crew, their mottled gray skin shining wetly in the flames, their webbed paws pulling the men over the sides.

He looked around for Joseph and spotted him emerging from the stairs leading to the captain's cabin, a revolver clutched in his hand. Henry shouted for him, trying to make his way around the flames, intending to make a stand at his side. He caught his first officer's attention at precisely the wrong moment; a large thin-limbed monstrosity opened wide its fish-like mouth, which bristled with needle-like teeth, and sunk them deep into his shoulder. Joseph fired one shot into the night, before dropping the revolver in agony. The creature wrapped its unnaturally long arms around him, its teeth still worrying at his shoulder, blood smearing its face, as it dragged him back and over the starboard bulwark.

Henry screamed in rage and anguish. The flames had created a semi-circular barrier, trapping him on the port side of the deck. There was no one to save, even should he manage to pass through the flames. He feared burning, but he now feared what might lurk in the water more. He dropped to his knees and waited for the flames. As captain, his failings would be absolved by fire.

And still, somewhere off in the distance, that inhuman wailing, an uncanny melody, sang out into the night.

March 1898

Chapter 1

Arthur

Casper, Wyoming

I sat on the small porch, overlooking the workers arriving to start work for the day. I sipped cautiously at my coffee, steam still rising from the cup on the unusually chill morning. Across the wagon trail, the frame of the house had started taking shape. I felt a gentle hand on my shoulder. "Good morning, Mrs. Wilson."

"Good morning, Mr. Wilson." I could smell her floral scent as she leaned down to kiss my cheek. "Ooh." She jerked away quickly.

I felt around my chin at the stubble there. "Sorry my love, I haven't shaved today."

"It's OK, it's what I get for marrying such an uncouth frontiersman." She moved to sit in the chair next to mine. We both sat quietly for a while, watching the workmen going about their business. Building a house. Our house. I glanced over at Catherine, blonde curls framing her delicate face, her eyes an almost luminescent shade of blue. I wondered how my life had ever come to this——this happiness.

We had met a few months before, in the midst of one of the most harrowing times I had faced in my life. I had felt myself drawn to her immediately. In an unlikely turn of luck, she had felt the same about me. She had nursed me back to health after I sustained injuries during a frantic defense of the town, and I had discovered in her a gentle soul with a piercing wit and intellect. As I regained my health, I also found myself falling deeply in love. A month and a half later, I asked her father's permission to marry. He gave it.

The following day she accompanied me on a wagon ride, to a spot I knew which had a beautiful view of the sunset. And as the setting sun lit the sky cerulean and violet, reflecting its rays off the waters of the Platte River, I got down on one knee, and with a nervousness I had never felt in the face of violence, proposed to her. To my delight and amazement, she accepted. I recalled that day now, and still felt in a dreamlike state whenever I looked at her. As though something was always looming, waiting to take her and my happiness away.

This, I swore would never happen.

I was nearly 40, but still in good physical condition. I had been a skilled marksman before the events of last fall; my time spent straying in different Frontier towns had given me a great deal of experience. Even still, I practiced at every opportunity. And not just with pistols.

When in town, I would listen with great interest to tales from veterans of the war. Occasionally, Indians would pass through and if they'd speak to me, I would ask them about how they employed their weapons. In most cases they would react with bemusement, but some were overjoyed to demonstrate their prowess at martial skills. There was even an old timer who claimed to have hunted Comanches with the Texas Rangers. I took it all in.

After all my friend Benjamin had saved us all, not through skill as a warrior, but with his tremendous erudition. I would never have access to the volumes of forbidden knowledge that his wealth and network of contacts granted him. However, I could fight. And I would 'til my last breath.

"You're remembering again." Her voice lifted me out of my reverie. The concern evident on her face.

"It's nothing. Just wondering if we could put a rampart and some cannon about the place."

Her laugh was musical. "It wouldn't match the salmon paint, or the windowsill lilac gardens."

I reached for her hand, felt her warmth as our fingers intertwined. She was one of the very few who knew what had really happened that night. We had concocted a tale of disease and madness, and most people had believed it. She'd been at the bedside of many wounded and dying men that night and heard their ramblings. And so, she asked me for the truth. It had been a pivotal moment. I chose to tell her the truth. I'd rather lose her to it than a lie.

She didn't react as I had feared. She listened patiently and when I finished, questioned me on specifics. I was amazed. When Benjamin visited from time to time, she quizzed him as well. This caused much consternation and some inhibition on his part. I enjoyed watching my scholarly friend as he was flummoxed by this beautiful woman. After a while they became friends, and he had been the best man at my wedding. He departed back home to Massachusetts, the discoveries here in Wyoming informing his research he said, and he must get back to his library. We said our goodbyes, with mutual promises to visit each other.

The sounds of construction rang out, another day closer to a new home, and Catherine's excitement made me excited for her. We were living in a cramped cabin that the county had provided, but Sheriff Patton would be leaving office soon and my position was in doubt. I had a reasonable sum of money saved. After all, there was little enough to spend it on all these years. Catherine's father insisted on building the home for us. I objected, but in the end, she brought me around.

And so, here we sat, a comfortable silence between us, as I drank my coffee and she watched the construction with bright eyes.

Chapter 2

Benjamin

Salem, Massachusetts

I re-read the critical part of the telegram: *Whateley wreckage found. All hands feared lost.*

The writing blurred and I realized my hands were shaking. I set the telegram carefully on the mantelpiece. I felt behind me and locating the Queen Anne chair I knew to be there, sat heavily upon it. I had warned the captain of the risks to be sure, but that his death, and the deaths of his men, were on my head was without doubt. The intent was for Captain Watkins to sail the defined route, matching the known time and places and note any aberrations. Such a large and well-equipped ship should have had no problem.

Since my encounter in Wyoming the year before, my esoteric studies had met a new terrifying reality, and I should have prepared them better or gone with them myself.

I clucked my tongue, foolish thinking. I would now be just as dead. I had needed Watkins to verify my suspicions, and once the verity of them had been established, I could come up with a plan to exact vengeance for my parents. Now what could I do?

It was at moments like this that I deeply missed my sister Abbie. She had gone to her grave with the belief that our parents had died in a boating accident, wrecked upon shoals in a storm… There was one person I could have shared these events with. Someone who would believe the truth about what had happened to my parents. But he was half a world away and had finally found some happiness. I could not disturb him for a personal vendetta. I would have to resolve this alone.

Although I had told Abbie that I remembered little about the accident, in truth, I remembered everything in grotesque detail…

The strangely dark skies, without a hint of rain. Our small sailing boat lurching to a stop, grounded upon some inexplicable basaltic rock. And then——a horrid fishy smell, which preceded the aberrant humanoid things that came over the side. My father trying to use an oar to drive them back, my mother's piteous screaming, pulled by her hair over the side. A wail of fury and grief from my father. I, petrified with fear, precariously leaning against the gunwale, as far as possible from the horrific things. A strike from the oar hitting my shoulder as he swung, knocking me overboard. Looking up through the turbulent water, barely making out my father gesturing and shouting. As my head broke the surface, I saw him disappear under a mass of figures, heard their hideous braying and croaking, made all the worse by a brief guttural utterance not unlike human speech. I swam then, in terror and shame and grief. Certain I would feel webbed claws dragging me down at any moment. At some point, I lost consciousness.

A lighthouse keeper on Bakers Island had found me lying unconscious on the western shore. Serendipitous.

After months of lying in bed, kept docile with morphine, I finally began to regain my composure. I managed to convince the doctor and my sister that I was well, the things I might have said, the ravings of a delirious man. I was soon well enough to assume the role of the family patriarch, and after all the stresses and grief, I was glad to take on the responsibilities so that Abbie could have her chance to mourn and rest.

That terrible event had set in me a new determination. I swore I would never fall victim to cowardice again. I had never been a brawny specimen of a man, but neither was I weak. I trained as I could with firearms and exercised regularly. But my finest weapon would always be my mind. I began to manage my inherited wealth carefully. My father had a number of shrewd investments. I multiplied them. Always with an eye to what benefit they might bring to my endeavour. I established a network of contacts who were able to acquire rare and unique items. Already the beneficiary of a classical education, I set my mind to learning obscure and dead languages. I deciphered occult tomes and practiced precise rituals.

So absorbed had I become, that I failed to notice just

when my sister had become ill. She, who had supported me during our worst hours. And in the midst of my industry, she offered her help with the bookkeeping and readily took to any other tasks I would ask of her. Her mind was as great as my own, her heart larger. Unobserved by me in my single-minded purpose, she had grown thin and wan. Through it all she had smiled, and her joyous spirit kept me from growing completely distant from humanity. Then one day, I passed her room, and saw her furtively turn away. I playfully asked if she was hiding some token from a suitor. I was devastated when she slowly turned, the front of her white dress spotted a bright crimson. I knew immediately what I had so blithely failed to notice before. I held her to me, heedless of any danger to myself, and she sobbed, the resolute facade of happiness at last shattered.

I frantically sent for doctors as far away as Boston and New York. They were useless. I sent to Europe for tuberculin, knowing the controversy, but desperate to save her. I refused to send her to a sanatorium. I tended to her as she had once done for me. I had been too ill to attend the funeral held for my parents at the time, and Abbie now insisted that I promise to visit their graves every month. I promised, as I would have promised her anything. She would give our butler instructions, insisting that he look after my health, knowing my research too often distracted me. Her concern for my wellbeing, continued even in her ailing state, was too much to bear.

Towards the end, during one of her moments of delirium, she spoke about creatures coming from the sea to take her. I knew it was just the fever in her mind, randomly fabricating thoughts, assembling words that she had heard me speak long before. Still, I was horrified. During those last days, she often would wake, terror in her eyes, drenched with sweat, only calming when she saw me beside her. As painful as it was, I continued to stay by her side as she struggled on.

Then, one morning, as the daylight had just begun to paint its yellow light across the walls, Abbie opened her eyes and spoke in a weak, plaintive voice, "Mommy...daddy." I held her hands tightly, as if to hold her spirit in place, but she closed her eyes and her breathing slowed and finally, stopped.

After the funeral, I threw myself even more into my work. I felt as though those horrors had taken both Abbie and my parents from me. Oliver stayed true to his word, and would make sure I took meals, and the occasional walk around the grounds. I kept my promise as best I could and visited the cemetery, where Abbie now lies next to the markers of my absent parents. I would fail in that promise at times but would try and make up for it with additional visitations, as if she was in the heavens keeping count.

Years later, I would attend an auction in Newburyport. They were selling books in a lot, most in poor shape, many with water damage, making them useless to collectors. I had a contact at the auction house who had looked over the books at my request and discovered that a few were partially legible. Etched on the inside board of one, a name—O. Marsh. Given the condition of the volumes, I was able to purchase the lot for a low price.

Weeks went by as I deciphered incoherent scribblings and tried to make sense of text made indecipherable by the damp. It was the discovery and translation of a ledger of dates and symbols that finally led to a breakthrough. It paralleled information I had obtained from other sources. One of those dates was the very same day in February that my parents had been murdered, and the Whateley lost at sea.

I pulled one of my journals down from a shelf. This too had a series of dates, and next to them, projections for the forthcoming astrological aspects. My finger traced its way down the list, and then stopped.

May 7th. I had some time to prepare.

Chapter 3
Walking Hawk

Big Horn Mountains, Wyoming

Walking Hawk crouched down at the sudden noise in the brush ahead. He motioned for Moo'soone to follow suit. It was known that the white man would likely kill them on sight. He was one of a few among his peers who defied the tribal elders and left the Northern Cheyenne reservation. Moo'soone was his brother and would not stay behind. Where once his ancestors lived and hunted, they too would live and hunt. They had fought and won many battles, and now peace had been bought with surrender. The shuffling up ahead only served to remind him that they were two men against the entirety of the white nation.

Their position behind a fallen pine provided them with more than enough cover. The men would not see the pair even if they were to walk a few feet away. They would observe, let them pass, and then follow to make sure they would not return. These mountains were tall, and deadly to those who did not know them. The snows could hide any number of dangers. The brothers knew every path, and many places to hide. The U.S. government had recently declared this a public land. This meant little to them, only that they could hunt without fear of encountering occupied homesteads.

The noise continued but did not change direction. His initial thought, that it was a white man or men given their inability to move with stealth, was now in doubt. Perhaps it was some predator savaging its meal. A great cat, or perhaps a bear wandering from its hibernation. He carried a Henry rifle passed down from his father before his death, a source of great pride and sorrow. His brother chose to use a bow, an arrow already nocked. He also kept his spear slung, quickly accessible if needed for the close work. He smiled and signaled him to move behind him. He would exercise caution, but not show fear. He inched closer, thankful for the fresh snow which was soft and would help them stay undetected.

The peculiar sounds were emerging from a tightly grouped copse of evergreens. He was now close enough to see where a few had been disturbed. Where the boughs widened towards their base, they had shed their cloaks of snow. Some few of the branches were still moving, this in spite of the windless day. Part of him now urged withdrawal. He would not heed it. Spotting a gap in the stand where he might observe whatever was causing the movement, he cocked the hammer on the rifle and began making his way silently around towards the break in the foliage. He signed to his brother, "Find cover". Should the trees conceal men, they would leave without a sound. If it was a predator, then they would need the skin and meat.

Only after he saw his brother in position, nearly hidden behind a white birch, did he move forward. He led with the barrel of his rifle. He knew the big cats would move like lightning. Careful not to disturb the branches, he used the rifle to push aside a thick needle filled offshoot and leaned forward to see into the nearly cave-like darkness created by the snow-clad firs.

As he waited for his eyes to adjust, the musky scent of animal and the acrid smell of blood reached his nostrils. He moved the rifle from side to side, looking for the thing he could hear snuffling in the darkness. All his senses were alert, and he became certain that a shape, a darkness within the dark, was where the noise originated. He slowly and silently moved his rifle to the right, to take aim at the figure, hoping to see it more clearly before he fired.

Too late, he saw the nearly luminescent yellow glow of eyes to his left. He swung the rifle back, quickly now, heedless of the noise and motion. He felt an agonizing blow to his jaw that spun him around, sending his father's rifle flying out of reach as he fell forward into the snow. He was light-headed from the power of the blow, but he raised his head to warn his brother. He could see Moo'soone's face, and the look of horror there. He tried to move his jaw to speak, and it was only then that he saw the thick blood in the snow, his blood. He reached for his face, and with a shock discovered that his hand touched nothing below his nose.

He felt an inhuman grip on his ankle, and could only wave his arms in gesture, pleading with his eyes. *Run, brother. Please run.* And then the trees closed over him.

Chapter 4

Arthur

Casper, Wyoming

I sat down at the table and poured some coffee. I got up early to get ready to head down into town, but Catherine had been up before me. I took in the smells of coffee and sawdust—and for the first time that I could remember, I felt comfortable in my time and place.

I watched as Catherine took swatches of cloth and held them up against the kitchen window. She turned them this way and that in the early morning light and made little tut-ting sounds as she did so. As she stood there, in the gentle mote-filled light, I felt that I had never seen anything more beautiful.

"What are you looking at?" She knew I was watching but continued her evaluations.

"Well, I'm sorry ma'am, I hadn't realized that it was now illegal for a man to look at his wife in Natrona county, and me being a deputy sheriff and all."

She turned to me, her blue eyes flashing. "You know I don't care for that country rube act. You are New England born and raised, and a college graduate."

"Yes ma'am." I turned my attention to my coffee. I felt her eyes on me for a moment more before she returned to her endless search for the right curtain material. She began to hum, a low tune, and in spite of the coffee I began to slowly drift off.

Her humming stopped. I looked up and saw her hand go to her breast. Her attention was drawn to something outside the window. I reached for my sidearm but realized my gun belt was still hanging in our bedroom. An instant later, there was a shattering of glass and wood as a dark gray appendage sunk into her chest with a meaty thud. My heart felt like it had stopped. Get up damn you! I shouted in my mind, but I was unable to move. I could only watch as the limb twisted and churned, an unearthly substance, alive, but not of our world. Then her head turned awkwardly towards me, her beautiful blue eyes now darkened pits, charcoal excrescences in constant motion. No...

"Arthur?"

I startled awake, Catherine's arm gently shaking my shoulder. I looked up into her eyes—her striking blue eyes and breathed a shuddering sigh of relief. My hands dropped to my revolvers, their comforting grips solid beneath my hands. She looked at me with concern.

"It's been some time since you've had a nightmare."

"Yeah, I know." I quickly finished my now lukewarm coffee. And got up to pour another.

"Do you want to talk about it?" She came up and wrapped her arms around my waist.

"No. No I think it's better to just forget it. It was just a dream. Probably brought on by this terrible coffee."

She pulled her arms away and gave me a quick jab in the side. "Well then, next time you can make it yourself."

As I turned around, she still looked disquieted. I placed my hands on her hips and kissed her deeply. She leaned into it and for a moment the dream was completely forgotten.

"See that's all I needed, a kiss from a pretty lady." I was rewarded with another jab.

"Any pretty lady?" She pretended a pout.

"Only the prettiest." She accepted my compliment and returned to the pile of small cloth by the window. I looked out and saw nothing but the plains grass of the foothills and the occasional sagebrush. "Do me a favor, keep the shotgun handy today. I'll feel better about it."

She looked at me for a moment, then moved to the bedroom, returned with the shotgun. I watched as she broke open the action and deftly put two shells in place, and quickly closed the break. She then walked past me and leaned it up against the kitchen counter. She looked back at me. "Good?"

"Very good." I smiled in spite of the lingering dread brought on by the dream. I sat back down and resumed drinking my coffee, my gaze drifting often, past Catherine, to the field outside the kitchen window.

April 1898

Chapter 5

Benjamin

Salem, Massachusetts

I called for Oliver and received no answer. It being early afternoon, I guessed that he must be in the greenhouse.

It was fashionable to collect rare orchids, and my parents had assembled a collection unique to this part of the country, and perhaps in the entire United States. I had no interest in floriculture, but Oliver had taken an interest after my parents passed, so I left him to it. I would make additions, purchased off adventurers who docked in Boston, as a token of my gratitude for his service. And I had to admit, they were fascinating to look at.

I descended the spiral staircase and entered the east hallway. The house was nearly maze-like in its design. I had failed to ask my father why he had it constructed so; as a younger man it had never occurred to ask, and now I would never have the chance. I recalled my boyhood in England and concluded that my father had likely tried to incorporate aspects of the old family manor in its construction. Perhaps, I could locate the firm that had designed it and speak with the architect...

I walked north, passing mostly closed and locked rooms, their contents left covered and abandoned since the loss of my family. I turned right at the small orangerie occupying the northeast corner and passed through an anteroom before arriving in the garden room where I exited to the rear grounds and the greenhouse there. My footsteps echoed in the large house. I had, at times, thought of moving. Perhaps even traveling to the west and joining my friend Arthur there. But found that I could not leave the family home. My fondest memories were here, and if all I had now were ghosts—so be it.

Another consideration was that the home now held my sanctuary. A wine cellar during my parents' lifetimes, it now served as a shelter and a study. It was ritually and physically fortified against malefic entities. It also contained, or confined, the more dangerous tomes and items in my collection. As of yet, it had not been put to the test, so it was a last refuge based on conjecture only.

I opened the double doors onto a beautiful New England spring day. Everything was vividly viridescent. The sky was clear, but there was the smell of rain. I stopped, and for a moment, a line from Tennyson came unbidden to my mind. I recited it to myself, *sotto voce.*

"*Why lift the veil, dividing. The brilliant courts of spring— Where gilded shapes are gliding. In fairy colouring.*"

I wondered what verses Tennyson would have made, had he encountered the things that I had seen?

I pushed through the introspection and started a brisk walk to the greenhouse. As I neared it, I did indeed see Oliver there, lovingly tending to a beautiful violet specimen, *Arethusa bulbosa*.

I stopped for a moment, silently observing Oliver. He had been with my family since before I was born. I had been terrified of him in my youth. He had an implacable demeanor and would chide me in that clipped British accent, seeming to have an uncanny ability to locate me wherever I might hide. My parents were the liberal sort, so I never got the hiding that some of my peers experienced, but he always managed to frighten me into compliance.

Only once had I seen that facade break. When I had tried to terminate his service. He plead his case, and I had conceded. Without the man the place would probably be desolate and decrepit. And here he was, treating a plant as gently as a child. I felt oddly voyeuristic, as if I was watching something intensely private. I knocked on the glass, to give him a moment should he require it, then entered.

"Good morning sir."

"Good morning Oliver, these look lovely, don't they?"

"Yes sir. I appreciate the most recent addition. I've never seen its like."

"Yes, *Cattleya walkeriana*. It's found in the higher elevations in South America apparently." I moved to look at the orchid in question. Such a delicate thing. "You remember

Mr. Walker? He was looking into an archaeological find for me and was kind enough to remember your fondness for orchids. I was glad to facilitate it. You keep this place looking like my parents might come walking in the door at any moment."

There was a brief, awkward silence. I wasn't sure where the thought had come from, though recent events had kept them often in my mind.

"Is there something I can help with sir?" Oliver set down his various gardening implements and began toweling off his hands.

"Actually yes, I have made some recent changes to my will."

I thought that I saw one eyebrow lift almost imperceptibly.

"Should I die, the house and the grounds will be left to you." He immediately began to protest, but I continued, unwilling to be deterred. "You're as close as family to me, and the other Hathornes have no need for more wealth and properties." I paused, an orchid catching my eye. The beautiful flower seemingly alight with an internal glow. I forced my gaze back to Oliver. "Of course there is a stipulation."

He was a moment in replying. "Yes sir."

"I've asked that a portion of the grounds be set aside. To become a public park, to be dedicated to Abbie. I leave it to your discretion as to which part will serve. I hope that is satisfactory?"

"Yes sir, but—are you sure sir?"

"I'm sure. With any luck I won't be going anywhere anytime soon, but should the unexpected occur, I can't imagine anyone else who would better take care of the old place."

He looked a little lost, and it occurred to me then, it wasn't just the place he was used to looking after, it was me as well. I was the last of our family, and he had been with us most of his life.

"Now, I need to ask a favor. I have a small package in the study that I need sent by courier. Once that has been completed, I will need some help in packing. I will be making a short journey by ship."

There was a slight twitch, the only break in his reserve. "Yes sir, but are you quite certain? You—dislike ships."

"I'm positive, it will be a short journey, hopefully no more than a day, should the weather cooperate."

"Where will you be going sir?"

"I plan to sail to the location where my parents were killed, Oliver. I need answers." I looked to the clear and cloudless morning sky for a moment, then clapping his shoulder, I gave him a wink. "And this time I will be prepared."

Chapter 6

Arthur

Casper, Wyoming

I headed south down Durbin, heard the sounds of the children playing in the schoolyard. A few of them saw me and waved. I tipped my hat, to the sound of their giggles. An almost perfect spring day, except for the wind. It gusted, driving gritty dust into my eyes.

I had stopped by to see Sheriff Patton this morning. He'd not been the same since the night of the battle last winter. He had always been hard as nails, and at times a difficult man to work with, but I admired him. He had stood up and rallied the town against the inexplicable. We all had scars from that night. Now it looked like he would end his term this year, and I had to decide what to do.

A small whine came from inside my jacket. I reached inside and gave a pat to the small furred head there. I was looking forward to Catherine's reaction to her new friend. I had made a side trip over to the Manchin homestead, having talked to Ed a few weeks back about the litter he was expecting from his Aussie shepherd. He'd kept a puppy aside for me, an adorable little fellow with a soft coat of gray and white and tan, and intelligent bright blue eyes.

I rode slowly, holding him to my side. The town, a raucous place at the best of times, had been relatively quiet since the troubles. Between Benjamin, the sheriff, and myself, we'd concocted a story at the time that we thought would best let the town sleep at night. But the men who had been at the barricade that night had seen the nightmarish reality. Some more so than myself. I was taken out of the fight early, and it was during the aftermath that Catherine and I had furthered our acquaintance.

I cantered along the wagon road into the foothills. The road itself would continue to snake its way through the foothills and up the north slope of Casper Mountain. The wind blew harder here, and I pulled the brim of my hat down, but the dust seemed to come from all sides. I moved my jacket as best I could to keep the grit from irritating my little companion. He seemed content to snuggle against my side, curled up in the cotton cloth that I had used to create a makeshift bundle to hold him.

After passing the third switchback, I could see our new home. It was a small place by New England standards, but out here it was mighty fine. So was the woman I could see on the porch waiting for me. I looked down into my jacket, "I hope she likes you pup."

I watched as she stood and waved. Ordinarily I would have brought the horse to a trot for the last bit of road, but the surprise guest made it awkward. As I got closer, I could see her concerned expression. I pulled the right side of the jacket back, giving myself clearance should I need it. I rode right up the trail to the porch, looking about for any signs of a disturbance.

"Good evening darling, what's got you upset?"

She looked up at me, one hand on the horse. "Nothing that can't wait for dinner. You took your sweet time getting here."

Realizing that there wasn't an immediate threat, I spent a moment figuring out how to dismount and keep the little shepherd a surprise. It simply wasn't possible, not without the both of us taking a spill, so I just reached into the bundle at my left side, and carefully extracted the little guy.

"Surprise." I offered the furry bundle to her.

She made an "oh" sound that I barely heard and took him from me. She pulled the cotton back to fully expose his furry head, and I realized that those blue eyes were nearly a match for hers. She looked up at me with tears, and I quickly dismounted and hitched the horse to the porch railing. I came around with my excuses ready. "I'm sorry. I thought with me gone most of the day that you'd like some company, and he'll make a great guard when he grows some."

"You idiot, I love him. He's wonderful. Does he have a name?" She was holding him face to face and he started giving her nose a lick. She giggled.

"No, least not that Ed had said. I thought you'd like to name him." I was both relieved and tremendously happy at her happiness.

"OK. Well, I'm going to have to give it some thought." She turned and kissed me deeply. "Now, you get that horse settled and come get some dinner."

There was a sudden change to her mien. "I had visitors today. I'm not sure if I should be worried yet or not, but we need to talk, so be quick."

I unhitched the horse and gave it a pat as I led it by the reins to the small barn behind the house. My nerves were jangling now. I got the horse settled, then hung my jacket from a nail and headed to the house without it. I wanted free access to the pair of Colts. Something was off.

I walked in the back door and latched it after me. It led into the kitchen and I could smell the tantalizing scents of the recently cooked dinner. I suddenly realized just how hungry I was. I walked through into the small dining room and watched as she massaged an old blanket to create a makeshift bed. The pup sat next to her, chewing on what I believed was one of my socks. Once she settled him into the little nest, she came to the table.

I said grace, and dug in. I looked up with a mouthful of the delicious stew, and saw that she was watching me, her bowl untouched. I continued chewing and gestured for her to speak.

"Around noon I heard horses coming up the trail to the house. I grabbed the shotgun and went to the door. I opened just the top and saw two Indians. They just sat a-horse and looked around like they were lost." She looked out the front window, recalling. "One talked to the other, and then he turned to me and asked if this was the house of Arthur Wilson."

She looked at me as if this advent was all my fault. I continued to shovel in the stew. If we were going to fight, she wasn't getting any of my bowl back.

"I said that it was and asked them what they wanted you for. They talked amongst themselves in their language some more, and then the man simply said that they needed to speak with you only and that they'd return."

This caught my attention. I finished my bite and asked, "When?"

There was a knock at the front door. She turned to me. "I would say now."

Chapter 7

Benjamin

Salem, Massachusetts

It was an early morning, with a light fog moving slowly over the calm seas. Looking at the details in my journal once again, I failed to see what I might have missed. There was a nagging voice at the back of my mind, suggesting that this was absurd, I was engaging with powers beyond the understanding of man.

I encouraged myself by recounting the fact that Arthur and I had faced similar horrors in Wyoming and had defeated them. Or at least deferred the threat to another day. This was different. I believed these were beings that were originally men. They could be killed the same as any man. That, at least, was my hope.

I was slowly getting used to the lulling motion of the clipper ship. Physically at least. Even here at dock, I felt the need to look over the side, expecting to see abhorrent shapes clambering up, gripping the bulwark—but no, there was only dark water, lapping at the hull. I forced myself to watch the bowsprit, using it as a mental focal point to calm and gather myself. There were only a few sailors, the other five men were mercenaries I'd hired. It was a small ship for a clipper. I had significant wealth and investments all over the world, but I could have wished for even more. A ship with the size and pedigree of a USS Constitution might give me some comfort.

I checked my revolver once more, a Smith & Wesson Model 3 chambered in .44 caliber. After the encounter in Wyoming, I decided that my pepperbox pistol was impractical, and that something larger and more efficient was required. I had seen the ease and skill with which Arthur used his pair of Colt's and decided something similar was required. Months of practice had followed. I was as expert as I could become in the time allowed. In addition, I had a Baker 10-gauge shotgun slung over my shoulder. The sailors had made comment on whether I might make practical use as an anchor. I didn't mind, drowning might be a pleasant end to this expedition.

I was afraid that the unpleasant truth was that man, and all his creations were insignificant. The ocean alone was unfathomable, to know that it was also home to eldritch monstrosities—well, then it became no little dread even to be near the shore. I was determined to overcome this fear, and to the extent possible, determine just what had killed my parents, and exact justice. I had seen the things with my own eyes—and yet part of me still wanted to deny the possibility of their existence. Madness lie in the realities.

The captain came on-board and gave my hand a vigorous shake. It was damp, and I had to fight the urge to wipe my hand on my jacket.

"So, we're ready? We should take advantage of the fair weather." Captain Hodges was a short, rotund man, and had wild auburn hair that framed a red, splotchy, and weathered face. A result of excessive drinking, I speculated.

"I'm ready captain, set sail at your leisure."

I watched him turn and give orders to the small crew. Soon the morning was alive with the sounds of a ship preparing to sail.

I glanced over at Thomas Griffin, the leader of the group of mercenaries I'd hired. He was a serious older man, a Civil War veteran with a steady manner. He was of average height and had short dark hair that had turned mostly gray. He was talking quietly to the group we'd gathered over the last few days.

I had hired a group of men who'd likely murder me and throw my body overboard, just for what little I had on me. It was likely a combination of Mr. Griffin's leadership, and the promise of even greater reward at the end of the voyage, that kept them honest. Word had it that Thomas had too thoroughly enjoyed his occupation in the war. I was counting on it. That they were mostly desperate and violent men well served my purpose.

I found myself wishing that Arthur was here with me.

The combination of his skill at arms, and his humor would not go amiss on a day such as this. He also now knew something of the unnatural. Perhaps, out of all the people in the world, he was the sole person I could trust not to break should we encounter those unnatural things that had slain my parents. In the end I did not request his aid, but I did send a letter explaining my purpose, in the case that I did not return.

"Sir?"

Caught up in my thoughts I hadn't heard Thomas approach. Now that we were under sail, was not the time to let myself be distracted. I replied, "Yes, Thomas?"

"The men are ready, though a little concerned."

"What are their concerns? Perhaps I can set them to rest." I suspected that, in truth, only Thomas had concerns, the rest would care only about payment.

"What are we facing exactly? You've said you believe that there are a group of pirates lurking out near this reef. They murdered your parents and you've hired us to exact revenge. That's understandable enough. The thing is, you're on edge." He paused to spit over the side. "Now, I've asked around about you, and I've been told that for a scholar, you're quite the hard man. So, what could have this man spooked, I thought? Then, I started asking around about this reef. Now, seaside taverns are abundant with tall tales, but the things I've heard over the last few days are the tallest. It got me to thinking. That maybe there aren't any pirates."

I turned to face the man straight on. "Thomas, is this really important? I'm paying you handsomely for your service. Does it matter what your men point their firearms at?"

"In fact, it is. Maybe not to them. But for this little adventure I'm their leader, and you could say I feel a sense of responsibility for them. I saw strange things in the war. It did things to my mind after, and it took a while to sort out. I believe there are things out there that aren't what you would call natural. So, tell me what it is that we're really after. If they aren't prepared, they'll break and run."

"And where will they run to Thomas?" I sighed. These were things I had not discussed with anyone and saying them out loud felt like a tremendous intimacy. After a moment's thought, I decided to acquiesce. There were already too many lost souls on my conscience. "The truth of the matter is somewhat difficult to believe. I kept it from you, not to put you at disadvantage, but simply because most men would likely believe me mad."

"Go on."

I gathered my thoughts. How does one explain the unexplainable? "We were attacked on the water. But not by pirates. Things, monstrous creatures, came out of the water. They killed my father and mother in moments, and I... I survived only because I swam away in fear."

I could see his jaw working as he appeared to consider what I told him. "Were you armed? Did any of you try to fight these…things, off?"

"No. It was meant to be a short sailing trip; of the type my family had done often. Usually only out to the islands and back. My parents were adventurers, of a sort, they knew ships and had faced dangerous seas before. This trip, my father spied a reef, which had drawn his attention, and he sailed closer for a look. We were set upon unexpectedly, and by things none of us had heard of, let alone seen."

"So, you believe they can be harmed, else why would you be here with us?"

"I do. I researched the phenomenon, and like you, visited many a tavern. Some who sail these parts regularly, have heard tales, and some have even claimed to have seen these creatures. Their descriptions matched well with my recollections. I also have a journal, acquired in Newburyport, that contains an incredible account. I also believe that the attacks follow a certain seasonal cycle. My hope is that this will be an exploratory expedition, not a battle."

"And we're here in case it turns into the latter?"

"Indeed."

Seemingly satisfied with this more detailed and truthful account, he wandered off with a thoughtful expression.

I turned my attention to the bowsprit once again, having felt both a sense of embarrassment and an unburdening, after speaking so honestly about my encounter with Mr. Griffin. I watched the morning sun begin to burn the fog off the water. I remained unmoving, even as the occasional ocean spray bedewed my face.

From now, until I set foot once again on shore, the ocean and all its horrors would have my complete attention.

Chapter 8

Arthur

Casper, Wyoming

I signaled Catherine to get the shotgun, as I got up from my seat and headed to the door. I kept my pistols holstered for the moment. They spoke with her earlier, so the old fear was set aside for the moment. Had they meant harm, there would have been no knock.

We'd had a Dutch door installed at my insistence, one of the very few architectural decisions that I had made. Knowing that Catherine could open just the top half should visitors arrive in my absence gave me some small comfort. As I passed him, the pup gave a small whine from his position in the blanket. "Hush boy, it's alright."

I opened the door fully. Knowing that should there be trouble I could draw and fire more easily. Two men stood in the fading light of dusk. The older of the two stood in front, facing me with his hat in both hands. He was dark skinned, his face deeply lined, gray-streaked hair tied into a thick ponytail, eyes dark and striking. He wore a traditional suit and carried himself in a way that strangely enough, reminded me of a minister.

"Hello, Mr. Arthur Morgan?" He spoke in accented, but concise English.

"Yes, I am. How may I help you?" My eyes darted from one to the other, assessing whether they had weapons, and trying to gauge their intent. The younger man was lithe, his hair long and straight, and he wore a light calico shirt with a dark vest, buckskin pants and moccasins. He wore a knife at his belt, but if they carried arms, they had been left with their mounts which I saw had been tied to a tree several yards away.

"I am John, and this young man is Moo'soone. We have come here seeking your aid. Will you allow us to speak?"

I glanced back at Catherine, and she gave me a slight nod. Neither of us sensed a threat from these men. Should that change, I still had my pistols, and her a knife, secreted upon her person. "Of course. Come in please. We were just eating. Could we offer you some dinner?" I stood aside and gestured them in.

John declined politely, but Moo'soone gave me a quick nod. He had the look of someone who hadn't eaten in some time.

"Have a seat please." They both took seats at the table and Catherine went to fix another plate. "Does he speak English?" I nodded towards the young man.

"No, he is Cheyenne, but he does understand a little. I was Salish, but was taken in by missionaries when younger, and took well to the language. Now I move amongst the tribes, sharing my medicine. And so, he came to me seeking help." At this he shrugged. "Our people are still struggling to come to terms with our situation. Some, like this young man, do not believe that we should be constrained to small parcels of land. They live in the wilds. The high uninhabited places. They travel silently and are careful not to draw attention."

I had taken my place at the table, and once I saw Moo'soone digging in with a relish, resumed taking small bites of my now cooling stew. "So, what brought you to me?" Catherine had taken her seat and seemed pleased with the eagerness with which he attacked his bowl. The shotgun lay against the wall within easy reach. Her concealed caution made me want to smile with pride.

John seemed to take this all in with equanimity. He looked at the young man with a sad smile. "I learned of you through a Shoshone. I believe he was known to you as Inkton'mi?"

I nodded, and at the mention of the name, my appetite ceased. I set down my spoon and pushed the bowl away. Catherine took it up, and brought out another bowl for Moo'soone, who had devoured the first bowl. He looked at her gratefully and resumed eating.

"I knew him. Not well, but I was there at his end."

John nodded, as if I had confirmed something that was

already known to him. "He was well known to the people. He had no true home, but was welcome among our people, as well as by the other tribes. He was known to be a very wise man, and he knew powerful medicine. He would help those who needed it and would only take drink or food in return."

I nodded for him to continue. I did not mention that the Inkton I knew tended to go heavily with the drink when he was in town. Knowing now what he had encountered in the mountains, I expected that it was only Catherine's presence that kept me from sinking into the bottle for comfort as well.

"He came to me some months ago. He seemed much changed since I had seen him last. He looked to be resigned. He was looking for one of tsétsêhéstâhese, our people. He had apparently ridden with a band of us many years ago, and I think he'd hoped to reunite with this man. He did not find him, and at the time, I couldn't help." He paused as Catherine set cups of coffee in front of each of us. "Thank you."

He took a sip and looked pleased. Catherine's father had mercantile interests in the area and always made sure we had the best coffee he could obtain. He was my favorite father-in-law for this reason.

"I didn't get to know him as well as I would have liked."

He nodded, as if he already knew this. "After he could

not locate this man for whom he searched, he said he planned to find you. He said that if anyone else could help it would be you."

I paused with the cup just starting to touch my lips. I couldn't understand how Inkton could have known much about me. We'd had few encounters prior to that fateful last night. "Did he tell you how he came to this conclusion?"

John shook his head. "At the time I didn't think to ask. As I said, it was believed that he had powerful medicine. He said he had one last great task that would be to all of our benefits if successful, and that to complete it, he would need your fighting skills."

I looked over at Catherine and found that she was studying the old Indian intensely. I began to wonder if Inkton hadn't had some insight into what would happen. Certainly he couldn't have intended to die? "So, what brings you, and your young friend here, looking for me?"

He looked at me for a moment, and then, as if a decision had been made, he began to speak. "I later found the man he had been looking for. I'm not sure he'd have been recognized, had Inkton'mi managed to discover him. He was old and frail, not at all as he'd been described to me. I heard from him the tale of what happened to him and his brothers in these mountains. Not long after, I came here to see what had become of Inkton'mi. I could not find him. And so I dared to go to that place, fearing that he had returned there. The mountainside had collapsed, and no sign of an opening remained. I believed that he had accomplished his goal, with your help, and died in the process."

He gazed at me, waiting for me to confirm his suspicions. I simply nodded. There wasn't much to be said. Certainly nothing that I cared to relive.

He nodded, satisfied. "Then it is true." He looked to the young man, now looking well sated. "Moo'soone deeply distrusts the white man, and so it was only the loss of his brother that brought him to me. When we began to lose others in a similar fashion, I learned what I could of what it is that we face. I am not a warrior, but I remembered Inkton'mi and the thing in the mountain, and so I come to you to ask for your help."

My mouth was dry, but when I looked at Catherine, she nodded encouragement. "What is it that you need my help with?"

He leaned forward; his lined face starkly lit in the light of the table lamp. "When young Moo'soone came to me with his tale, I believed it was just the hó'nehe, the wolf. I have now seen the remains of one who went to hunt it. No wolf could do that to a man. I thought, perhaps the vo'estanehesono. The little people. Then I saw the tracks. It is something else. Something we have no name for. But perhaps something you have."

***

Our guests having departed, Catherine moved about the small kitchen with an almost frantic energy. I stared down into my mug; the coffee there having long gone cold. John had promised to return early in the morning for an answer, and I mulled over what we had been told and wondered at the vagaries of fate that had led the men to me.

From the corner of my eye, I could see Catherine drying the dishes with what seemed like an excess of toweling. I rubbed at my temples, trying to delay the inevitable. I had an overabundance of bad choices awaiting me. I could go north with the two men. Determine if some remnant of the thing had made its way there. And then, hope to slow or destroy it somehow. Or I could wait—and hope that there was some simpler explanation, and destruction wouldn't overtake us in the days and weeks ahead.

I couldn't find it in me to choose either option. I had a deep, paralyzing fear for her which made the choice impossible.

"So."

Her voice shook me from my reverie. "So."

"Arthur." She slowly turned, and I saw the tears in her bright blue eyes. I stood and walked over to her, took her in my arms. "I really don't want you to go."

Her voice came to me, muffled from her place on my shirt, "Who else can fight this but you?"

"I can't leave you here, not alone. Not at the foot of

these mountains. If this—thing is the same as what we faced before, who's to say it's not coming here too?"

She was quiet for a moment. "I would go stay with my father. Eleanor is probably fed up with him and could use the help. And... I think he's been lonely."

I clasped her arms and turned her gently to face me. "Benjamin isn't here. He's the only one who really has an idea of what these things are. Without his help, we'd never have fought them off before."

"Then ask for his help. He wouldn't refuse you."

I considered it for a moment. There was still an awkwardness between us. He had been the better friend, though he wouldn't say as much. When he left, he said that he had family matters to attend to. Given that he had no family left, I wasn't sure what that meant but it must have been of the utmost importance to him. "I'll go and scout it out. Patton owes me some time. If it looks to be anything like what we encountered here, I'll send a telegram to Benjamin. Even if he's unable to come himself, he may be able to provide some guidance in the matter."

"Then we have until morning." She met my eyes with hers, bright and wet from tears. I took her by the hand, and we made our way to the bedroom. There, we made love with a newfound intensity, made up of our fears, our desperation and our hope that tomorrow would not come.

Despite our best efforts, morning did arrive.

Chapter 9

Benjamin

Atlantic Ocean

The rank smell of fish was overwhelming, and my mother's cries tore at my very soul. And yet, I couldn't move. It wasn't fear that held me this time. My body simply didn't respond to my commands. I looked towards my father, oar clenched in both hands, fighting these creatures of nightmare as though it was a regular occurrence. Then-he looked right at me and nodded. As though we had previously agreed on some matter, and he was now confirming it. Still unable to move, I watched, as again the oar struck my shoulder, sending me over the side....

The falling sensation continued, and I awoke to discover that I was sliding down against the side of the gunwale I had been resting against. I was startled wide awake, and with a rapidly beating heart, I quickly regained my balance. I took a quick look around the ship to make certain that no one had noticed my gaffe. Such a time to fall asleep!

I quickly returned my thoughts to the nightmare. These sorts of dreams were nothing new. Most always repetitions of the disaster; self-guilt and its effect on my psyche. But now something had changed. I tried to gather together the wispy threads, before ephialtes quickly fled leaving me with only vague shadowy glimpses of distorted memories. One thing alone was I able to grasp with certainty, and this thing I would not let go of. In this instance of the recurring horror, my father had very clearly looked at me and nodded. And the blow from the oar which had sent me over the side—had been intentional.

I desperately sought to determine whether this was an actual recollection, only restored after all this time, perhaps by the associations of this trip—or was it merely some phantom of my subconscious.

I looked out into the murky fog which had grown heavy over the dark waters. The captain had reduced sail and was now conducting soundings. I began to grow more anxious. I periodically withdrew my hands from their tight grasp on my revolvers and shook them to keep them loose. Should the unthinkable happen, having stiff hands during a firefight could prove fatal.

This was meant to be an exploratory expedition, and I had made sure that we arrived here well before May eve. Walpurgisnacht. A date that I had learned held importance to the cult that worshiped here. Well known as an important date for sabbath to the witches of Europe, I had wondered at its significance here. Regardless, my hope was to find the reef quiet and empty.

The journal I had acquired mentioned the need for

sacrifice at the reef twice a year. Did those things which resided there come out only on certain auspicious dates, or were they always there, and the sacrifices merely kept them quiescent? I strongly hoped for the latter.

The clipper continued to slow, now nearly at a full stop. I could see the dark water over the sides, thick fog obscured it beyond a few yards. The sun was a veiled yellow orb, its dim light giving the scene a surreal quality. The only sounds, those of the ship. The crew spoke in hushed tones as if they could sense the wrongness here. One could almost believe that we had stumbled into some netherworld.

I tried to shake loose the overwhelming dread and glanced around the ship. I saw Thomas, carefully checking his weapons, his men talking quietly nearby. Even the most boisterous of his motley crew were subdued.

I carefully walked towards the bow, avoiding the various accoutrements of a sailing ship. Though I had sailed often with my parents, my father had handled the rigging, and since I had expressed no interest, he hadn't sought to inform me of their various purposes. I regretted that now, like so many things.

The Captain was now at the fore talking quietly with the sailor conducting the soundings. I stood quietly, knowing they'd both heard my approach. The sailor slowly let the line out. I saw that the line had small, marked leather wraps at regular intervals.

The captain half turned towards me and pointing to the line I had been observing, remarked, "Those are fathom markings."

The line had stopped, the leather marking a barely visible "7" just above the water line. The captain hastily turned and began bellowing to his crew. I tried to pick up on the parlance, but it made little sense to me. What was clear, was that we were stopping. I turned back to the sailor who was pulling in the line. He sensed my questioning look, and without turning from his work, began an explanation in surprisingly refined speech, so different from most sailors I had met in my travels.

"Seven fathoms. Roughly. So, perhaps 40 feet. Much too close to our keel. Based on the charts that we do have of this area; this should be deep water." He turned to me, and I saw his face in full. He seemed a very young man, with fine details and bright green eyes. "We may have found your reef sir."

"Thank you. I had best go see to the men." He nodded and returned to his work, but I was already lost in my thoughts.

My stomach churned with anxiety. In the silence of our passage, time had allowed me to analyze my feelings. For years, I had berated myself for failing to do anything on that long ago day, but now this daydream... Or memory? With my destination now close at hand, I had begun to hope that the things which dwelled here slumbered in the deep. I needed more time. And I needed to speak with Oliver, to discover what he might have been keeping from me all these years.

Thomas was speaking quietly but sternly to his men as I approached. As I neared, he finished speaking, and I saw the men scatter with their rifles at port arms. He took up a position next to me, and we both watched as they took up positions to cover possible boarding points, weapons now ready to fire at anything that should come from the water. The sailors watched them warily. I wondered what he had told them.

"We have reached the reef. Perhaps. It seems to be a matter of some uncertainty."

Thomas surveyed the fog-covered surrounds. "The weather certainly doesn't seem to be in our favor." Using the barrel of his rifle, he pointed towards the dark waters. "It's of no matter, if something shows, we'll see them in time. And the men are ready." He gestured toward the men patrolling the ship.

"What have you told them?"

"Some of what you told me." I started to protest, but he continued. "I made it a bit more palatable. Sailors and mercenaries are both a superstitious lot. They are eager to believe such tales, and even more eager to tell some of their own. The trick is in the telling. Too much and they'll be overcome with fear, too little and they won't take the threat seriously."

I realized he was correct. Should this trip be for naught, they'd have tales to spread about a foolish dandy hunting sea monsters. That I could live with.

Suddenly, the sun came out from its shroud, and in the bright light of day, the men and sailors looked about. Some for landmarks, others for potential threats. After some few minutes the fog began to disperse. There was some muttering amongst the crew. I could not follow the sailors' logic in finding sunshine to be an ill-omen. The same overall quiet that had accompanied our journey thus far continued unabated, even with the change in weather.

A shout came from the crow's nest, and a moment later the bulk of the crew were trying to see over the forecastle. I moved up, Thomas at my side, to discover the captain already there, looking through his spyglass. He handed it over to me, and raising the glass to my eye, I guided it toward where he pointed. To the north-east, easily visible with the aid of the spyglass, I could see a dark mass of land. Unlike most of the natural sea hazards along this stretch of coast, this one seemed to have been thrust up alone from the depths by some torturous cataclysm.

I watched as light waves washed up against the reef. As the waters rolled in and out, there was an occasional glimpse of a darkened grotto. It appeared that reef was littered with small caves.

I turned the glass westward toward the shoreline. I was somewhat astonished to see that there was a small coastal town located there. I rifled through memories of the coastline as I had seen it mapped and could recall no town here. Perhaps it was abandoned. It certainly seemed barren of life, and those few buildings that I could make out were in states of dire disrepair.

Removing the glass from my eye, I swung it again to the reef, and once there found it in the eyepiece, traced its outline downward, until it became merely another dark shape under the dark and undulating waters. As I carefully moved the glass, I felt an overwhelming sense of vertigo and suddenly the view was in motion through no agency of my own. The dark waters viewed from my one observing eye became everything.

Down and down, through murky depths pierced through with shimmering curtains of light. And I traveled deeper still, until those sheets of light gradually faded away and the waters turned grey around me. Though I could see little, I had a sense of motion, as if objects or creatures were darting just out of sight, following me in my downward traversal. Gradually light gave way completely, and I found myself in an abyss. The sense of descent ceased, and although I could see nothing, there was a deeply disturbing sensation of mass in front of me. I could not bring myself to move in this otherworld, afraid that should I reach out my hand, it might touch—something. Then, before me, a viridescent horizontal line appeared. So close as to seem blinding in the blackness. It grew slowly wider, revealing itself not pure, but mottled with striated variations of color. A frantic screaming began in the back of mind. The light grew in width, as if ponderously large shades were being retracted, and the screams grew to a cacophonous din in my head as I fought maddeningly to pull my view away....

I felt hands pulling at me and with a shock I came back to my full senses. I realized I had moved perilously close to falling overboard. The captain and Thomas were both looking at me, the one with concern and other with what I could only describe as curiosity.

I carefully handed the spyglass back to the captain, trying my best to conceal the shaking of my hands.

"I apologize captain. I think perhaps I overestimated the fitness of my sea legs for this journey."

The captain nodded slowly but seemed satisfied with my answer.

"What would sir like to do now?" I could not discern the nature of the look Hodges favored me with from under his brows.

"Please set anchor here, I'd like to take some notes and make sketches."

The captain nodded and moved away. It seemed that most of the crew had become more boisterous and less ill at ease over the changing of the weather. Thomas had been standing quietly, alert but also watching the reef curiously.

I withdrew a notebook from my valise and began quickly sketching the reef and what I could recall of the town as I had observed it through the spyglass. The effect of the strange vision on me made it difficult to concentrate, but I was determined to capture what I could of the layout of the place. There was certainly something awry here.

"Here we are at your mysterious reef and yet, you seem in a hurry to depart. My men and I haven't yet been engaged."

I glanced at Thomas. His gaze was now drawn towards the shore, and he seemed to be able to discern something of what was there, even without the aid of the glass. I spoke as I sketched. "Familiarity breeds contempt? At any rate, something has occurred to me. A recollection." I paused for a moment, the images still crystal clear in my mind. "I believe the answers I'm looking for do not begin here."

Sketching the reef was quickly done, at least that part of it that could be seen from our present location. Although logic said it was simply a formation of rock, there was a peculiarity to it that discomfited a person. And I could not overlook my earlier reaction to it. I turned towards the coastline and began sketching what I could recall of the town there. Taking an occasional look in the distance, I was able to add in some landmarks that might be helpful should an overland trip became necessary.

"To be honest Thomas, you have also engendered confidence by your professionalism and behavior whilst onboard. I feel more secure knowing that our defense is in capable hands should the need arise."

"I'm glad to hear it. Though you might want to wrap up your drawings a bit more quickly. It appears that someone has taken an interest in us from the town there."

I glanced up carefully and gazed over in the direction that I saw Thomas looking. It took me a moment, but then I saw it: sunlight reflecting brightly off a small surface. Very likely the lens of a spyglass, much like our own.

"Indeed." I returned to my sketch, trying my best to give the outward impression that I was unconcerned. "I will hurry. If you could tell the captain that we will be ready to return to Salem in a few minutes. I can continue my work as we sail."

He stood facing the town for a moment more, and then began heading to the stern to pass on my instructions. I overheard him stop and give one of his men some quick command, before continuing on his way. Struck by a sudden apprehension, I hurriedly sketched. The beginnings of movement from the ship were not enough to ease the burgeoning fear that my racing mind had created.

Interlude

Innsmouth, Massachusetts - April 1898

The cloaked man held out his hand for the spyglass. The hand which delivered it into his palm was malformed and had a moistness to it that the man found repellant. He pulled his kerchief from a pocket and wiped down the glass before placing it against his eye.

He located the ship almost at once. Although the men aboard her were little more than small shapes at this distance, he believed he knew which of them was the man he was seeking. Agents in Salem and elsewhere had been following his movements, and he had received an urgent missive just that morning that the last Hathorne would be onboard a ship sailing for the reef. He had set out for Innsmouth immediately and managed to arrive just a few hours before the ship had been spotted.

He returned the spyglass to the clammy outstretched hand. The glass disappeared into the many folds of the rags which covered the hunched form. The man, for it was once a man, looked up at him with large unblinking eyes. "Will they come here?" It said with a thick strange voice interspersed with glottal sounds.

The cloaked man looked down at him with unconcealed distaste. "No. I have seen to Mr. Hathorne. We have the friend being observed as well. Mr. Hathorne we know. The other is a curiosity. Perhaps Benjamin shall tell us about him before he dies."

The response he received was a grunt that was likely approval, and with that the figure started walking awkwardly towards town, the tattered cloth obscuring whatever deformity slowed his pace. The cloaked man looked out at the outskirts of Innsmouth, where the buildings sat in the early stages of disrepair. Although unfortunate, these things did not matter. He returned his gaze to the reef. Below it, deep in the abyss, a wondrous kingdom awaited. He need only serve it.

Chapter 10

Little Owl

Northern Cheyenne Reservation, Montana

Little Owl crept just outside the firelight. From his vantage point he watched as a small band of Cheyenne gathered near a wagon, bartering quietly with a trio of white men. He knew that the wagon was full of liquor and weapons, all goods which were forbidden for trade. He hadn't been old enough to remember when Little Wolf went into exile, but he'd heard the stories throughout his young life. He wondered what the current Chiefs knew of this exchange.

He spat. They were all cowards. For what they were. For what they'd done to him.

He had always been different.

Early on, his mother and father had believed that his strangeness was a sign. It was. Just not in the way they had hoped. On the hunt, he became wild. Began to revel in slaughter and bloodshed. Soon he was hunting alone. He sought out the old one who told tales of the beginning. He would sweat in the lodge and cut strips of his skin from arms and legs, offerings to the spirits. He believed that if the tribe would only return to the old ways, they could take back the land of their fathers. Bloody the white man in such a way that they would only think of them in terror. One morning he awoke to a small pile of owl feathers, and whatever their provenance, he'd taken to wearing them proudly. He became Little Owl, a name he treasured. He would likely never have another.

He maintained his position, watching as the negotiations grew heated and voices began to carry. Overheard from where he lay prone in the undergrowth, a debate over the quality of weapons on offer. One voice spoke commandingly above the others, and they quietened. Now boxes were handed down from the wagon. The sounds of lightly clinking glass carried, making their contents apparent. He then saw two long bundles passed quickly from the wagon, into the waiting hands of their buyers. Those with the bundles quickly scattered into the night.

He knew finer weapons still lay hidden in the wagon. They carried a high price. He'd make it higher.

He had heard many things in his unseen ramblings. There was something hunting in the forests and the high mountains that would take men or animals and was said to be invulnerable. An angered spirit said some. A diseased animal said others. It was of no matter to him. He would kill it. And leave its carcass in the middle of the reservation. They would not see him, but they would know that Little Owl had come through like death in the night.

***

He ran through the underbrush, parallel to the wagon trail. When his sight was obscured by trees or rocks, he continued on without hesitation. He knew where they would go, and even had he not, the noise made by the white men would have made it simple to track them regardless. He began to move faster, knowing that the wagon wouldn't be able to compete with his speed as it traveled down the rutted trail.

He slowed as he neared the place he was looking for. A small glade, gently lit by moonlight, which opened to the left of the trail. A dark circle in the midst of the crushed grass surrounding the area, made obvious the remains of previous campfires. He remained in the dense trees and brush on the right side of the trail and looked about for signs that anyone, or anything, had come near since he'd last come to this place. There was some old scat, and nothing else. No sign that his hiding place had been disturbed. No recent spoor from predators.

Little Owl crept to a large fallen tree, overgrown with age. There he walked along the trunk to a spot where a hollow in the tree had combined with a depression in the forest floor to create a cavity large enough to conceal his lithe form. He crouched down and retrieved his weapons, left here earlier in the day. Once so armed with axe and bow, he curled into the space and pulled loose brush in to cover his position. There he waited.

Hours passed before his patience was rewarded. The woods fell silent, and Little Owl assumed a position of readiness. He flattened his hand on the earth beneath him, feeling for the subtle vibration of an approaching wagon, but it lay still beneath his hand. From his hidden place he looked out over the glade, where the moonlight created moving shadows over the uneven ground as it passed through the trees which swayed in a sudden wind. He thought he saw movement near the tree line, but the motion either ceased or was a trick of the light.

He felt a prickling along his skin, and he forced himself to become even more still. His instincts told him that there was danger nearby, and he prepared his bow with an economy of motion. As he scanned the tree-line for signs of movement, he heard voices, speaking loudly and carelessly from the direction of the wagon trail. The potential predator in the trees was ignored, it would no doubt leave as the clamorous traders came closer.

He watched the woods through which the trail wandered, and after a few moments he could see the yellow glow of lantern light as it flickered through the branches. The boisterous voices became even louder as they neared. He silently scoffed at their carelessness. Soon the wagon and its sole outrider rode out into the open, filling the formerly serene space with a dull light and the noise of men and horses.

From his location, he observed the outrider dismounting near a lone aspen and hitching his horse there, roping the mount to the oddly curved trunk. Little Owl had passed the tree many times. He believed that if a tree could feel pain, then this one had suffered long. He looked again for the shadow amongst the trees, but shadows abounded as the white men went about setting up camp in the light of their lanterns.

For some time he watched them as they made a fire in the well-used spot and began to drink heavily from their own wares. He had anticipated needing to quietly eliminate at least one lookout, but soon all three men were settling into their bedrolls. He nearly snorted in his contempt. With so much liquor in them they'd die easily and without a fight.

Little Owl stretched his limbs out slowly to change position. A cramp now would hamper his speed. He expected the men to drop off quickly to sleep, but two of them talked loudly. Occasional gales of laughter rang out in the hollow. It appeared he would need to wait a little longer. He crawled upward and into a patch of thick grasses, lying prone to observe them more closely. With the light from the campfire, they would be blind to his movements.

As he began to rise, movement in the tree-line caused him to freeze in a half-crouch. For a moment he thought perhaps it was the firelight creating the impression of movement, but then with a stab of fear he saw the firelight gleaming briefly off a gibbous yellow orb in the darkness. He almost moved in his alarm but caught himself and forcibly stilled his body.

Now he could clearly follow the thing as it moved in and out of the trees with a strange sinuous, halting gait. It was hard to make out its form; one moment it seemed to lope, wolf-like, then it would *flow* into an upright position. It was almost hypnotic, and for a moment his focus was wholly absorbed, becoming oblivious to his position and surroundings—and then the horses began to nicker with agitation.

He shook his head, forcing his eyes down and away from the *pull* of the thing. The men had mostly quieted, and when he looked up, he could see the one closest to him was rising noisily from his bedroll to go check on the horses. His eyes darted around, looking for *it*—then a scream arose from the edge of the camp and he found it at once.

Little Owl sat in his concealed position, watching as the interlopers were slaughtered in ways he couldn't have imagined in his many glory-filled dreams of vengeance. He felt no fear of the thing now. This was clearly the creature that had killed his people, but it was no wolf or bear; not a thing described in the many stories he had so avidly absorbed. This was something else entirely.

As it finished with the last man and beast in the glade, it paused; and from within the seething mass of the thing, a single inhuman orb looked right where Little Owl was crouched watching. He felt as if his heart had stopped. The yellow eye almost seemed to luminesce, and it was if something passed between the two and then it was off, moving incredibly fast for something with such an uncanny means of locomotion.

Little Owl took in a deep breath, and then stood and walked over to the dying fire. What lie scattered about the camp did not make up enough to have been three men and their horses. He looked into the dark undergrowth in the trees, where the thing had disappeared, and began to follow.

Chapter 11

Arthur

Casper, Wyoming

The sun's subtle glow had just begun to dull the neighboring stars. At Catherine's insistence, our bedroom window had been set to face the east, and I had been watching the skies for what had felt like hours.

I silently crept downstairs and headed to the stable to saddle Herodotus. A black Morgan that Benjamin had bought, ridden for only a few days, and then bequeathed to me before returning to Salem. It was typical of the man. He would never flaunt his wealth, he simply found it to be a means to an end and seemed unaware of the attraction it might hold for others.

Moments later, John arrived alone for my answer. I suspected that I was being watched as we spoke. He seemed unsurprised by my intent to travel with them, and I bade him await me at a designated place north of town. He nodded his assent, and I walked Herodotus towards the house, to where Catherine had been watching from the doorway. She waited until he had disappeared into the tree line, and then stepped outside, carrying a small cloth bundle.

"For the trip. Just some things that I thought you might miss."

"Coffee?"

She smiled. "Coffee too." Then tears began to well, and I quickly grasped her to me. We said our goodbyes and as I kissed her, I took the moment to breathe in everything about her.

"I'll send word to your father when I reach town."

She nodded, and after a final embrace, I mounted Herodotus and began the ride down the wagon road that led into Casper.

***

A little over an hour later, and I was cresting a small ridge and quickly spied the two men. They were waiting, as arranged, on the north side of the Platte, in a spot where it forked a few miles west of town. I had suggested the location to John earlier, believing that we should not draw unwanted attention by riding through town, and he had agreed. Both men quickly and silently mounted their horses. Moo'soone now had a lance and bow secured to his steed and was armed with two knives on his belt. John still looked the part of a minister, only now he had a variety of items nearly bursting from his saddle bags, and I spied the grip of a single revolver on his right side. I nodded, and we pointed our steeds north.

We ascended a very gradual slope which went on for miles, before reaching a point where the land spread out in waves of hills before us. I stopped for a moment and turned to look back. Casper was barely visible, and the mountain was completely obscured by dark clouds. It felt like an ill omen and I fought against my instinct to return immediately to Catherine.

Hours passed as we rode over small hills and through gullies, the ground covered in sagebrush and the occasional small cluster of trees. Now and then the prairie grasses would be dotted with wildflowers; white, yellow and purple clusters breaking up the monotony. Small clouds, moving across the sky, would briefly occlude the sun, and whole sections of the plains would grow dim, creating a constantly changing vista.

I believed we had probably left the county behind, but I had no way of knowing. At this point I was completely reliant on John, as I had no reason to travel this far north in the course of my duties and recalled only the vaguest details of the maps I had seen.

The quiet ride left me reflecting back on the morning. The sheriff had readily agreed to my leave but pressed me on my reasons. I had known that leaving a beautiful woman like Catherine, so soon after marriage, would bring questions. I had been questioning myself and didn't particularly care for the answers.

I was as honest with the man as I could be, given that I didn't know with any degree of certainty what it was exactly that I was going to investigate. I only knew that I had to be sure that there was not a part of that thing still loose in the world. And I needed Sheriff Patton to be extra watchful. Should it manage to find a way out of the tons of rock we had buried it under, he was the only one who could take action.

In the end, he promised to watch over Catherine, and would make sure that he or one of the other deputies visited some of the more far-flung ranches and homesteads more regularly for any indication of danger. He had also warned me. I would soon be outside of Natrona county, and therefore no longer under the auspices of his office. Should I run into trouble, he would do his best to help, but had limited influence. I assured him that I would do my best to avoid any incident which might bring the almighty power of the U.S. government down on us.

Thinking on this, I looked over to my companions. John had assured me that they had committed no crimes, and I believed him, so much as it mattered. I knew little of the affairs of the various tribes and had experienced no trouble with them myself. I had arrived in Casper well after Fort Caspar was in ashes. I saw the occasional itinerant Indians coming through town, or sometimes a group riding afar, but had given little thought to the matter. That is until I had met Inkton.

The old Shoshone had frequented the Grand Central, and for a time, I knew him as a harmless drunkard and huckster. His wrinkled face, with his deep twinkling eyes, always hinting that he knew something that you didn't. Now I knew that to be true. In one night, I learned something of the man. And lost both him, and my friend Crawley Harris.

I still dreamt of the thing that had been Crawley, and of the brutal killing of Inkton. All the machinations of some vast unfathomable alien intelligence. Or at least so far as Benjamin had explained it to me. For myself, I often worried that some part of those men lived on, and the horror of it was unbearable. I was not a religious man, but from time to time I would still send up an occasional prayer that they were both at peace.

I shook off those memories and tried to focus on the present. We were riding through a series of gulches, the ground a patchwork of sand, broken up with sagebrush and rock. A breeze had picked up, lending a chill to those moments when the sun was obscured. The wildlife here was typical of the plains; rabbits, prairie dogs and the occasional rattlesnake that found it warm enough to hunt.

At John's suggestion, we had decided on a plan the previous night. To ride west and then north for Ten Sleep. He hoped to receive more current news there, allowing us to formulate a plan before continuing on further into the Big Horns. The alternative was riding north and taking the old Sioux trail east across the Big Horns, which he said was more of a risk, given that we would have no intelligence before entering the mountains. Riding light, and for long days, should get us there in three days by his estimation.

Thus far we had been making quick work of the miles, only slowing when encountering the occasional prairie dog towns, which forced us to lessen our pace; to avoid the holes that could lame our horses. The cayuses that the Indians rode seemed to instinctively evade the dens, and I did my best to follow closely.

The sun was now directly overhead, and the day was beginning to turn warm. We settled into a companionable silence. Other than the sound of the horses, and the occasional buzzing of an insect, all was quiet. My mind turned inwards. I started thinking of the time it was taking to travel there, the time it had taken for them to find me, and how quickly the thing had nearly taken all of Casper. And I wondered if I'd ever see Catherine again.

Chapter 12

Benjamin

Salem, Massachusetts

I had fallen asleep, in spite of the lurching and clattering of the coach as it made its way from the docks to my home. I was startled awake by the gentle shake Thomas gave my shoulder. I opened painfully dry eyes, sore from the blowing sands encountered during our brief detour to Plum Island.

Earlier that day, as we had begun the return voyage, I had recalled that a source of mine had found certain materials on that island. In spite of my disquiet, I saw a chance to gain the rare blooms that I might soon require. Based on my notes, it was an auspicious time to gather them, as we neared May Eve.

Taking one of the two small boats, a small group of men joined me as I trudged through the sands of the dunes and made my way to the marsh. There, strange things would sometimes wash up and nestle in the mud and tidal creeks. I took a circuitous path that avoided the conical lighthouse. I had a sense of someone watching, ever since Thomas had drawn my attention to our watcher. I had no reason to believe that I was the focus of that attention, yet the fear remained.

Another two hours had passed before I felt that I had exhausted the island of its treasures. We made our way back to the boat and rowed out to the ship. From there our journey back to Salem was swift, the winds favorable.

A light cough brought me back to the present. Thomas was holding out my valise. I took it from him, and looked out onto the misty cobbled streets. I couldn't see anything unusual, and yet, there was still a feeling of being observed.

"Mr. Hathorne, I must confess I find myself at loose ends."

I turned to look at Thomas, uncertain of the meaning behind this declaration.

He pointed towards the house. "It's a large place and you seem to be a little spooked." I stiffened. "I thought that you could maybe use someone who's handy with a gun about the place."

I looked at Thomas as I considered his offer. His demeanor had not changed, and yet I now wondered at his easy acceptance of my story earlier in the day. I felt that I had established a certain trust with the man, and yet, this suggestion felt almost like coercion. Could it be that he was somehow in league with the very entities that I sought to eliminate?

He looked away for a moment. "To be honest, the lodging house is overcrowded. If you'd be willing to put me up for a short time, and contract me at a rate that's fair to both of us, you'd have yourself an extra gunhand."

I debated internally for a moment. My agents had delved carefully into his background and associates before bringing him into my cadre. He had no known associations with any criminal elements. And yet, how would one identify interactions with occult groups? Their secrecy was a hallmark.

I also had to consider that fear and fatigue were playing on my usually sound judgement.

My decision made, I took his hand, and shook on it. "Thank you, Thomas. I'll have Oliver prepare a spare room."

He did not smile, but merely shook my hand as if this was the inevitable outcome all along. Together we disembarked the coach and made our way up to the house.

***

Later, as I walked past the open door of the room Oliver had established Thomas in, I saw him setting his rifle against the wall. I knocked lightly, and he answered without turning.

"Mr. Hathorne?"

"Are you settling in well?" The room Oliver and I had chosen was but a few doors down from my own. It was close enough to serve should his services be required but would also necessitate his moving across a creaky expanse of flooring should he have other intentions. After some protest against the improprieties, Oliver also agreed to move into the room across from our guest.

He turned, and with a sweep of his hand to indicate the whole of the room, he replied, "To be honest, I'm not sure I can sleep in such luxurious accommodations."

"I'm certain I could ask Oliver to fetch a rat, and perhaps a flea or two? If that would make it more to your liking."

He surprised me by letting out a sort of hoarse chuckle at this. "No thank you Mr. Hathorne. Though if you find me on the floor, don't be startled. Ever since the war, I've found beds somewhat hard to sleep in." He gestured towards the rifle. "Will you and your man be armed?"

"Of course. Oliver prefers the simplicity of a shotgun, and I have my own defenses."

At this, his eyes narrowed. "Do you then believe that we might be visited by something other than men?"

"My hope is that we are not visited at all." I paused, uncertain of how much to share with this man, who still engendered some doubts despite my intuition about his character. "I confess that I've had the sense of being watched."

He grunted as he sat on the edge of the soft bed. "Trust your instincts. Mine are the reason I'm still here."

"Then I'm glad you are here to guard my person. I will be in my study for a while, I promise to scream loudly if I am attacked. I bid you goodnight Thomas."

He simply nodded. As I departed the room, he tossed a pillow onto the floor and grabbing a blanket began to settle there.

Oliver was waiting for me in the hallway. He had a 10-gauge slung over his forearm, breech open.

"It's been an exhausting day. Tomorrow we must talk. Good night Oliver."

"Of course sir. Goodnight."

I turned toward the stairwell, leaving a nonplussed Oliver behind me. I needed time to gather my thoughts, as well as go through my notes and sketches before I approached what would likely be a difficult conversation. Passing through the dining area, I picked up my satchel from the small table where I had left it earlier. I headed towards the doorway which would lead to the cellar. I had work to do.

Chapter 13

Arthur

Big Horn County, Wyoming

By the second day, the monotony of travel had begun to quell my unease. At least during the day.

Our gradual northern course had abruptly changed when, at midday, I spied some riders accompanying a wagon coming towards us from the west. John had seen them first. "Riders from Lost Cabin. Let's turn north here."

I followed as they steered their horses northward, and we rode on at a steady pace for the remainder of the day. We ate lunch in the saddle and only stopped when the lack of light made it dangerous for the horses.

Now that evening approached, the fears crept up on me again. There is a vastness to the plains at night, which one has to experience to fully understand. On the cobbled streets of my hometown, one can walk under gas and electric lights, the crushing bulk of buildings obscuring the surrounding country, dulling the stars. Man holds dominion there.

Not so on the plains. Under the dark and endless sky, one becomes aware of their insignificance. There are no buildings to conceal you from the abyss, and the land seems boundless and empty. Standing watch at the edge of the camp, looking up to the night sky, I felt as though I was alone, in all of existence.

"It is sometimes staggering to behold, is it not?"

John was early for his watch. It was becoming a pattern for the older man. "I suppose it is." I still remained looking outward from our small camp, "would you like me to stand out the rest of my watch with you?"

I sensed as much as saw the shake of his head.

"No thank you. I've grown old, I don't need as much sleep these days."

I looked at the man, his face all crags and shadows. "All the same, I'm not sure I can sleep just yet."

"Then I would appreciate the company." For a moment I thought he donned a sly expression, then it passed. A trick of the shadows perhaps. "It would be helpful if you could tell me more about your encounter in the mountains. We likely have a few more days before reaching our destination. But that could change if it has been moving south."

It was the last thing I wanted on my mind at this time and in this place, but I had been anticipating it all the same. Before I could answer, I heard the howl of a coyote, followed by a series of barks which carried in the distance. It set my nerves further on edge. "What would you like to know?"

He nodded, as if my assent had been expected. "As

much as you can tell me. How did it begin?"

I began to relate the nightmarish events of the prior fall, and he listened silently throughout, at times his eyes gleaming in the starlit night. For reasons I couldn't define, I left out only two details: Inkton's tale, and Benjamin's involvement.

I felt exhausted by the end and was ready for my bedroll. John was watching my face carefully in the gloom, and though he said nothing, I felt that he suspected that I had made omissions. "I should turn in."

He nodded. "You've given me a lot to think about." His hand fingered the small dark bag hung around his neck. "Goodnight Arthur."

I made my way to my bedroll and thought of Catherine as I lay there staring up at the stars. I thought, that when this was all over, I would like to lie with her under these very stars. With her beside me, I could face this indifferent immensity and see the beauty there. Fatigue pulled me into sleep. And perhaps it was because my last thoughts were of Catherine, but I slept soundly and without dreams of any kind.

***

The next morning, I awoke to the sound of voices. Speaking in their own tongue, Moo'soone was speaking with a hushed urgency, and although I couldn't make out what they were saying, I decided to continue the pretense of sleep in the hopes of making out a word or phrase that might allow me to determine the nature of their conversation. There was a pause, and then I heard John speak again, his voice taking on a dark, stern tone. Then silence, until I felt a hand on my shoulder, almost startling me into motion and spoiling my ruse.

"It is time to rise." John spoke quietly, in his more familiar tone of voice.

I got up with what I hoped was a sufficient amount of mock sleepiness. It wasn't particularly challenging, given that our cold camps kept me from enjoying the coffee Catherine had packed. White frost covered most of the ground about us, and with the sun just coming over the horizon, the ground all around glittered. As I rolled up my bedding, I could see my breath in the morning chill. I could not tell if this abrupt cold was due to the change in altitude or merely another spring day in Wyoming.

As I saw to Herodotus, I noticed that Moo'soone was already ahorse, and looking northward, his normally impassive face hardened with anger. I didn't know how much English he might understand and given the contentiousness of the overheard conversation, I was afraid to try and speak to him with John nearby.

The farther we traveled, the more uneasy I was beginning to feel about John. He was very secretive and possessive of the belongings in his saddlebags. I'd noticed furtive glances as he rummaged about in them. At first, I put it down to cultural differences, but now I began to feel that my suspicions might have some substance.

Moo'soone seemed to me to be nothing other than what he appeared; a young man torn by grief and a desire for vengeance. I could not speak his language, but I understood his feelings all too well. And now, there seemed to be some conflict between the two men that I was not privy to.

Given that we should arrive in Ten Sleep in just a few hours, I could only hope that whatever disagreement they had between them was not related to our hunt. In the face of this danger, there could be no dissension.

Chapter 14

Benjamin

Salem, Massachusetts

I awoke with a distinct unease, after having fallen asleep at the writing table. I listened for a repeat of any sound that might have brought me awake. Little sound traveled from the sturdy old house upstairs into the converted cellar, and yet I felt that some minute atmospheric change must have occurred which brought my senses into a state of high alert. I reached for the gun belt at my waist and my stomach sank as I remembered that I had left it in my bedroom after changing from the trip.

I looked around the room for a weapon, but there was little there of practical use; mostly books and alchemical devices, some rare or completely unicum. I glanced over to an escritoire and made a quick mental inventory of its contents. There was a moment of realization and I moved quickly to open one of the small drawers, reaching in for the small Remington Derringer. I seldom fired it, and the .41 rimfire rounds it fired did little to embolden me but having any weapon to hand was a comfort.

So armed, I crept up the stairs, moving stealthily and staying alert for any unusual sounds. I reached the door and quietly turned the key in the mortice lock, keeping a hand on it should I need to quickly bolt the door. I peered through the gap and into the darkened hall, pistol at the ready, and listened.

The wind had picked up at some point since losing myself in the cellar, and the trees surrounding the house were beating and clawing against the walls and windows. Oliver had turned off the lighting, and now only a dull light came in through the windows, and the wind-blown foliage created a kaleidoscope of shadows.

I was frustrated in my efforts to detect any unusual sounds as the howling gale rose and fell, but then I caught a scent...like the docks after the fishing boats have come in. It was the smell of the ocean and death, brine and offal.

I debated silently for a moment; should I shout for Oliver and Thomas and risk revealing my position or move quickly and quietly to their rooms and hope that I was not intercepted. My decision was made for me when I heard a crash loud enough to be overheard over the storm. The sound originated somewhere to my left and it made me hopeful that the west stairway would be clear. I had a chance to make it to their rooms.

I sprung from my position and ran, quickly realizing my mistake in not having removed my shoes beforehand. They clacked loudly on the flooring where rugs did not muffle my steps. It did not matter; I was committed to my course. I reached the stairwell and taking the steps two at a time I quickly reached the landing and pivoted on heel to climb the remaining stairs.

I took an inadvertent step back as I realized a figure stood above me, neatly disguised by the dim light amidst the dark wood and deep red carpeting. Only for a brief instant had the fluttering gloom alighted on the crablike hand, pale against the dark mahogany of the bannister.

It was wearing a mismatch of stain darkened rags which covered it from head to toe, and in that moment in which we had nearly collided, a face peered sidelong at me from within the cowl-like covering over its head and in its countenance were all of the remembered nightmares of my youth. I raised the small pistol without hesitation and fired.

All was now chaos, as the muzzle flash and smoke made everything even more obscure, and the thing in front of me let out a horrendous gargling screech which was answered by a series of strange hoots and grunts from elsewhere in the house.

I quickly put my back to the wall in the hopes that it was still holding the bannister and ascended the stairs, flinching as I felt the thing's damp garments brush against me. It was now leaning hard against the bannister, the loathsome smell that I had scented earlier was coming off it in waves. I passed it by, and a misshapen hand darted out; its nails clawing me in a failed attempt to grab my arm. I ran to the top of the stairs ready to yell for Oliver when I saw him exiting his room with shotgun in hand.

"We've intruders." I gasped out. At the same time, I saw the flash of gunfire at the end of the hallway, and I could barely make out Thomas firing his rifle towards the center of the upstairs hall, where my quarters were. It appeared they had ascended both stairwells, and therefore had us trapped. The sounds and smells were appalling, but I had no time to give them consideration as Oliver pushed me aside and fired his shotgun down the stairwell from which I had just climbed.

The booming roar of the gun was deafening, fired as it was so close to my left ear, and although I was disorientated by the chaos and confusion, I managed to feel along the wall for the light switch and depress it, and after a moment the soft yellow lights illumined the hall. Filled as it was with gun-smoke, it did little to aid my vision, but it was a comfort nonetheless.

I grabbed Oliver's shoulder, as he peered down through the haze into the still darkened steps. "Let's move back towards Thomas's position. If we can push our way to my rooms, I can properly arm myself."

He glanced down at the small derringer in my palm and nodded. I noticed he had one hammer still back on the shotgun, one shell between us and whatever lie downstairs. I guided him as he kept watch behind us and noted that Thomas was kneeling and sighting along his rifle but hadn't fired in some time.

He looked towards me with a grin. "Well boss, work started early."

"Indeed. What have you seen?"

"I'm not certain. It was dark and after hearing your shot, I came out to a racket and saw a pale face at the corner. It was…" He squinted as he paused as if struggling for the correct word. "It was standing there like a person, but what I could see of the face, didn't seem right."

I nodded; I knew all too well these things that had haunted my nightmares. "We need to move towards my room. If you can cover us moving forward, Oliver will guard our rear."

There were assents from both, and I began slowly moving down the hall with my two bodyguards. For that's what they had become. At least until I could reach my room, and the weapons I had foolishly left there. We only needed to move to the center of the hall, and pass through the doors on the right.

I flinched as another crashing sound came from downstairs, and Oscar looked back at me. "I daren't think of what damage they might be doing."

The strange vocalizations and noises the things made

had quieted somewhat and there were no more cries. I wondered if we had managed to kill some of them. Unlike the creatures I had encountered at sea, these seemed almost human. As if they were undergoing some sort of metamorphosis.

After a seemingly interminable amount of time, we reached the double doors to my rooms. I looked to either side of the hallway, but it appeared clear. "Keep your guard up, I'll be just a moment."

I quietly pushed down on the handle of each door, and they swung wide. I breathed a sigh of relief to see that there had been no intrusion here. Then I remembered, I had left the cellar door unlocked. I moved quickly to the desk and grabbed my gun belt, buckling it quickly. I drew one of the revolvers and moved to one of the windows.

The dim light cast a small glow on the nearby grounds, and for a moment I didn't see anyone or anything milling about, but then a pale face hove into view from where it had been hidden under what I now realized was a dark top hat.

A tall, thin man was standing there; perhaps had been for some time. Now that he was clearly looking directly at me, I stared in wonder. He didn't have any of the aberrations of the things in the house, rather he looked more like some gothic villain; dark hair, with a thin mustache and goatee. He carried a cane, which he lifted and pointed in my direction with a smile. It was difficult to see in the crepuscular light, but it did not seem a pleasant smile. I raised my revolver to aim it towards him, but taking a step backward, he was instantly lost to my sight.

"Damn!" I rushed back to the doors where Oliver and Thomas waited. "We need to get downstairs."

"Do you hear it?" Thomas had his head tilted, listening.

There was silence in the house, but one could just make out the faint sounds of a team of horses fading into the distance. I ran for the stairs, my protesting comrades quickly following on my heels. I made note that there was no body on the stairs, or the landing. It had either survived, or they took their dead with them. Once I reached the ground floor, I ignored the state of my belongings and rushed to the cellar door. I turned, "You both must stay here."

Thomas began to protest, but Oliver guided him gently aside with suggestion that they search the floor for any remaining stragglers. As they headed off, I took a deep breath and headed into the cellar.

The fishy stench was everywhere, and the damage to the items I could see was both enraging and heartbreaking. Here was my life's work. When I saw the bookcase, which concealed the doorway secreted there, had been crudely searched but not moved, I allowed myself a small, relieved sigh. I moved cautiously around the room, careful to avoid the various unguents, powders, and potions that had not escaped the devastation. It was surprising that nothing had exploded or caught fire.

In the midst of all the detritus I could not easily see what it was that they were after. Not everything had been destroyed, only incautiously cast aside in the search. I went to my desk, and upon seeing that the locked drawers had not been opened, I sighed with relief. The contents of the desktop were also scattered and so it was that I did not see the missing item at first.

A more thorough search of the area around the desk confirmed it; only the small statuette was now missing.

It had adorned my father's desk for many years, and with his passing I had placed it on my own. A horrific thing that had fascinated me as a child, had later faded into the decor as just another bibelot, and had now been taken. I needed to know why.

Chapter 15

Arthur

Big Horn County, Wyoming

We had left the low rolling plains behind the day before, and for some time the earth had been broken up by buttes ridged with pale red and the occasional singular rock formation. Moo'soone was able to instinctively find narrow trails through foothills veined with coulées. The range to our east seemed to have grown out of the hills around us, outdistancing its peers and growing to dwarf them all. I could now clearly see patches of green forested area and at a distance; the gray stone of the peaks creased with white where winter's snow remained.

John reined in once we reached the summit of the hillside we had been ascending, and I rode to his side. He pointed downward. "Ten Sleep".

I spotted a small cluster of wooden buildings in the valley below. A homestead could be seen nearby, the smoke from the chimney drawing my eye. John had explained that Ten Sleep had been a well trafficked rest stop for the various tribes. Now it seemed to have grown in permanence, though I wouldn't have ventured to call it a town.

Moo'soone started down the hill without a word and I followed, with John bringing up the rear.

It was slow going until we reached the valley, and then we were able to pick up some speed. It was another hour before we rode up, dusty and tired, to the small town of Ten Sleep. It wasn't much to speak of, A few larger, wood-cladded buildings, a dusty main road and a smattering of small houses. There were a few people about, most passing us by without a second look. I turned toward John.

His eyes scoured the mountain, as if he might spy the thing from here. Without turning to face me, he spoke. "I will find my scouts. Perhaps you and Moo'soone should refresh our supplies. Otherwise, we will only have what we can hunt on the mountain."

I nodded and dismounted as he rode off. Throughout the day he had an almost feverish look as he frequently glanced towards the mountains. It was during the day's ride that I had the realization that some dynamic between the three of us had shifted during our travels. Moo'soone had started sharing looks with me when John's attention was elsewhere. John, ever aloof, seemed no longer the caring ward. If anything, there had been a tension growing between them as the days had passed.

I looked around for a mercantile and spotted a small timber cladded building which looked like a possibility. Our translator having left, I could only turn to Moo'soone and make motioning gestures towards it. He instead pointed back towards a small copse of trees we had passed on the trail a short while before. "Come. After."

He turned his horse and made his way back towards the trail as I sat for a moment, stunned by hearing his only use of English since we had met. I pondered what this might mean as I took the reins and led Herodotus to a cross post nearby that I used as a hitch. Stepping up onto the wooden walkway, I kicked off the hard mud which had packed itself onto my boots. It had either rained in the last day or the ground here liked to keep itself damp.

Doffing my hat, I opened the door to the small shop. It looked like many others I had seen in crossing the frontier, only the addition of fine glass windows hinted at the grasp for a lingering existence. The shop owner had just added another 5lb bag of flour to the existing stack in a back corner before patting his hands on his pants and turning to me. "Ahem, help ya?"

"Just in need of some rations. Do you take post, or maybe have a telegraph?"

The shopkeeper was a short, rotund man, with carefully pomaded dark hair, liberally shot through with grays verging on white. His beard was an unconstrained and barely groomed mess. He wandered around the shop, looking at the arrangement of items before responding. His breathing seemed labored from his earlier efforts. "Post sometimes.

Ahem. Telegraph…ahem. Casper would probably be the closest. Ahem."

"I've just come from there, was hoping to send a message back if I could."

At this he stopped his wandering and looking at nothing in particular rubbed his bearded chin in thought. "Casper. Ahem. Something…" He went into a small cubby that was lined with a number of inexpertly crafted shelves and emerged with a parcel about the size of his hand. "Yes, ahem. Here it is. What's your name sir?"

"Arthur. Arthur Wilson."

He walked towards me with the parcel extended, "This is yours then sir. Ahem. Only arrived early this morning, and ahem, I had almost forgotten."

I took the small package, and immediately recognized my wife's handwriting. Why had she sent something here that must have cost a great deal to have arrived here before me? I untied the twine and removed the linen-lined paper which was covering a small wooden box topped by a piece of paper carefully folded into a square. I took both and settled onto the only small wooden chair in sight.

Unfolded, the paper turned out to be two sheets, one laid on top of the other. Each contained short letters. Catherine had arranged it so that I would see hers first upon unfolding it. I caught a scent of her as I read the beautiful flowing script with which she wrote.

My Dearest Arthur,

This post was waiting for you upon my arrival in town. Given that it was from our mutual good friend and arriving so close on your departure, it gave me a strong premonition that I should open it. Forgive me for reading your private correspondence, but I believe in this case it was warranted and know you will feel the same. I hired a rider at some expense to deliver it to you at Ten Sleep and can only hope it finds you there. Finish your work and fly home to me.

Love,
Catherine

I folded this letter carefully and placed it in my chest pocket. On the other piece I could see the lettering written in Benjamin's crablike and yet precise hand.

Arthur,

I have written this to you in haste as I am occupied with events nearer to home. And yet it would ease my mind to know that you have receipt of this box. I have scraped together enough materials to make some cartridges for those revolvers that you favor. I will not go into the detail of their making here, other than to assure you that they are in every way the same as those that worked to such great effect previously. In this larger caliber they may have even more puissance, who can say? It is my greatest hope that they are never needed and will serve only to provide the impetus for a "tall" tale for your future children.

Your friend always,
Benjamin

The content of the combined letters left me in a state of emotion that I could not name. I carefully folded Benjamin's letter and placed it next to Catherine's.

I felt a permanence in the end of Benjamin's letter that made me fear for him. I opened the wooden box and saw 12 cartridges, carefully placed in holes bored for the purpose. The lead of the bullets was covered in intricate and delicately crafted sigils and each contained materials I could only speculate at.

"Sir, ahem?"

I turned to the portly shopkeeper who had patiently sat through my examination of the box. "Yes…yes. I need a few things for trail rations. And do you have the materials for me to send a return letter?"

***

I walked outside and placed my hat back on to block the sun which was now almost directly overhead. Mounting Herodotus, I rode back the way I had come looking for Moo'soone and the group of trees he had headed for. I looked about for John but did not spot him here, on what seemed to pass for a Main Street in Ten Sleep.

A short ride to the spot amongst the trees, and I soon saw Moo'soone. He rose from where he had been sitting on the ground and raised a hand in greeting to me. I rode closer, dismounted and strung the reins over a low tree branch. Moo'soone walked to a more heavily shaded spot and sat cross-legged on the ground. I joined him, in a position more suited to my lack of flexibility.

He pointed to his chest and then to me and speaking in halting English said, "Me. You. Must talk."

I shook my head, wondering at the deception. "So, all this time you have spoken some English? Why hide it, and why speak now?"

"The beast. John, no kill." He said this with a slashing motion at the end. I could see that he was very agitated. I suspected this was either as a result of his poor English or the fact that he needed to speak it at all. Perhaps it was a combination of both.

I tried to simplify and slow my speech. "If we find it, I will kill it. John will have no say."

He sighed, looking relieved. It was clear that he could understand English better than he could speak it. I didn't know if he had learned some as a child and not used it, or had quickly picked it up, nor did I have time to puzzle it out. John could return at any moment. He patted the spear that lay on the ground at his side. "I will kill. My brother."

I nodded. This was a matter of family and pride and

I simply didn't have the time to explain what I believed we were up against. I could only hope that our combined efforts could destroy the thing, and that we both kept our lives. My slowly growing suspicions about John made me wonder, what could he be thinking? Was he some sort of naturalist?

"Why does John want to save it?"

Moo'soone spat. "His gods."

"His gods?" I didn't understand, but before I could frame another question, Moo'soone stood up and grabbed his spear and walked towards his mount. In a moment I realized why, I heard the sound of a horse on the path and turned to see John riding up. I stood, and he rode up to me. He stayed in his saddle, his eyes alight and feverish, almost unrecognizable from the man who arrived at my home some days ago.

"It is still in the mountains. It is close and moving south. If we take the old trail, we may be able to intercept it. Quickly now!" He spoke some words to Moo'soone, who did not reply.

I mounted up and urged Herodotus into a canter to follow John, who had already started riding westward through town. Moo'soone rode up alongside me. We exchanged looks and he nodded towards John. I nodded. If necessary, I would subdue the old man, his intentions no longer mattered. Moo'soone and I were here to hunt.

Chapter 16

Benjamin

Danvers, Massachusetts

I disembarked from the coach onto the gravel of Hathorne Hill; the name not without its ironies. Looking up at the massive façade of red brick with its decorative wrought iron dahlias, I found myself genuinely curious about the institution. Unfortunately, it was not the purpose of my visit. The building swept out; massive wings gradually stepped back from the center. The view from the hill was quite tranquil on this quiet morning. A vast change from the last few days.

In the aftermath of the attack, I had contacted my various agents as well as some professional colleagues, in a bid to turn up whatever information could be uncovered about the mysterious coastal town we had seen from the ship. It had been an exhausting few days. What little sleep I had managed had been filled with dreams that left me even more weary.

The nature of my dreams had also changed. No longer were they subconscious flagellations, twisted visions of the horrors from my past. I would awaken distressed and disoriented but could not recall the specifics of what had so disturbed me. And so, I put it down to the stresses of recent days and by way of cure, drove myself into constant action.

I had ordered Oliver to hire help in repairing and cleaning the home, though against his protests. There was simply too much damage and too little time to salve his pride. In the basement I had taken inventory of the destruction and set about putting things to rights.

The years I had spent fortifying it against the preternatural had proven completely ineffective. Only a bit of legerdemain had saved the most valuable items of my collection. It was the source of much consternation, as it meant that those creatures had been of a mundane nature. Possibly even human, or once so.

I had made plans to address that oversight. In the interim, I bade Thomas gather up what brave men he could find to guard the house. He had ridden off early that next morning and returned with five men. Two of whom I had remembered from the group he'd engaged for the ship.

With the immediate needs accomplished, I began the search for information which had led me here.

I knocked on the door and after a few moments was greeted by a matronly woman, who led me to the office of the asylum superintendent. As introductions had already been made by my colleague, I was warmly welcomed by

Dr. Harrington; a distinguished looking gentleman, slightly balding, with a well-kept mustache and spectacles. Taking my arm, he immediately began to lead me down the left hallway. The doctor explained that the men were assigned to the left wing and the women, to the right, with the more excitable patients kept in the farthest building of each. It was not lost on me that he was walking quickly through the first building.

"Where do you keep Jacob Edwards?" I asked.

He straightened his spectacles, "Your man was an enumerator on the 1890 census. A family man, and by all accounts as sane as you or I." He paused to open the door to the next building. As we entered the next hall, he pointed towards a set of double doors to the side. "Hydrotherapy. We're quite advanced here."

The hospital was not what I had expected. It was brightly lit and appeared clean. Dr. Harrington was greeted by the odd passing doctor or nurse, but the halls were mostly clear and there was very little noise.

It seemed to take him a moment to return to the conversation, as if he was mentally combing through the patient's records. "Of course, that's not how he arrived here. He was nearly unrecognizable to his wife and son, so great had the changes he'd undergone in the few weeks since they had last seen him."

At this, he must have caught my glance. "No, he's not

violent. Not generally." He was quiet for a moment, "Occasionally, during the worst storms, the winds bring in the salt water from the ocean and then...well he can get quite excited. You see it's the scent, or perhaps rather the idea of the ocean that terrifies him."

The next set of doors were already open, and we passed into the next building. It was mostly quiet as well, but there was more activity. Patients being escorted to one place or the other. I could see a group of them outside in the gardens, as we passed by one of the windows. The doctor began to slow as we approached the closed doors to the next building.

"Mr. Edwards is on a regimen of the latest treatments and should be quite calm for your visit. However, I cannot say how he will react to your questioning, so I would ask that you do your best to refrain from exciting him." He opened the doors, and now I could hear light muttering and moans coming from the rooms. "I'm not sure if my old friend Professor Steadman happened to mention one of the more intriguing aspects of his case?"

The professor had told me very little, and I said as much. I tried to ignore the sounds as we continued down the hall toward the waiting Jacob.

The doctor stopped and faced me directly. "There was a similar case some years back. Almost identical circumstances. In that case, I believe the man was a tax collector. He had gone missing for some days and had later been found ranting in the streets of Newburyport. He violently attacked some passersby and was shortly thereafter brought here for treatment."

I could not help my excitement, "Could I see him as well?"

He shook his head sadly. "He was transferred. I was at Bridgewater when he arrived there. He was uncontrollably violent. Unfortunately, he took his own life before we could find suitable treatment." We resumed walking and arrived at a door on the right-hand side towards the end of the hall. "Ah, here we are. This is our man Jacob."

I watched as he took a key ring and unlocked the door, opening it onto a small tidy room. There was a narrow bed against the right wall, upon which sat a slight clean-shaven man. His hair was dark and unkempt and hid his features, as he did not look up at our entrance. There was a small table and chair and little else. The windows allowed the daylight in, although it was somewhat dimmed by light clouds.

"Good morning Jacob. You have a visitor." The doctor spoke cheerfully and waved a hand towards me by way of introduction. "This is Mr. Hathorne. He would like to speak with you. Would that be alright?"

I watched Jacob for a reaction, but he merely scratched at his left arm. Dr. Harrington looked from Jacob to myself and motioned me towards the chair. It was modest and uncomfortable as would likely befit the conversation.

"Thank you doctor."

He nodded and left the room, shutting the door behind him.

"Mr. Edwards, I understand that you were an enumerator. Who was your district supervisor?" I watched for a reaction, but he continued to scratch, his arm now red raw from his ministrations. After a moment I realized that there was no easy way to broach a topic that, if overheard, would likely result in my internment in this very same institution. "What can you tell me of the last town you visited in the conduct of your duties?"

He began to scratch furiously, as if to dig underneath the skin and reach the sinews beneath, so I rose quickly and gently put a hand on his moving forearm. He paused and, in my haste decided to take a gamble, "I know about them."

At this he looked up into my face, and for the first time I could see his eyes. They were bright, a penetrating green, gleaming out from the dark and sunken skin around them. At one time he would have been considered handsome. Now however, the intensity of his gaze coupled with his physical deterioration would likely cause people to give him a wide berth should they encounter him in the street.

I realized that the arm I was holding had grown still and I slowly removed my hand, as if from a shying animal. He continued to stare into my eyes, and I held the gaze, ignoring my increasing discomfort. When he spoke, I almost didn't hear him, so quiet and rasping was his voice. "Innsmouth."

"Innsmouth." I kept his gaze and nodded, as if I had known the name all along and was also privy to its secrets. "I need your help Jacob. They…" I paused, a sudden tightness in my throat. "They murdered my parents, and I mean to put an end to them."

At this Jacob began to shake, as with palsy. He looked slowly away from me, his gaze becoming focused on some distant point in the daytime sky. After a few moments, his body stilled.

I slowly took my seat, careful to keep my demeanor calm in spite of my churning anxiety. It seemed that several minutes passed, and I was beginning to despair of his ever coming round, when he broke the stillness and in a halting and reluctant manner, he began to tell me of his visit to Innsmouth, and the strange and hostile folk he had encountered there.

Chapter 17
Little Owl

Big Horn Mountains, Wyoming

Little Owl had been sitting on a bed of pine needles and talus for hours. At present, the sun was shining on his resting place and he closed his eyes, feeling the warmth on his face. Now and then a chill breeze would gust, stirring the few deciduous leaves that lay on the ground.

The thing had entered a deep crevice just before dawn, a dark ring of blood, fur and other detritus outlining the entrance to where it now hid. Little Owl had followed it for many miles, to arrive at this spot at the border of the tree-line. A steep escarpment loomed above him.

His fatigued mind ran through the previous evening's pursuit, the exhausting venture testing even his skill and strength. At times he was forced to follow from significant distances, marveling as it scaled inclines that a mountain goat would find difficult.

He recalled the chill that had run down his spine at a rabbit's scream echoing in the deep night, the small creature somehow falling in the path of the quickly moving thing. It was the only such encounter. The forest was quiet, he heard only the blood pumping in his ears as he struggled to keep apace of it.

Watching the dark shape through night-adjusted eyes, he had struggled to put a form to it; it shifted in ways that hurt his head if he focused on it directly for too long. As the night passed, he developed a certainty that the thing he followed sometimes took on the shape and gait of a great wolf.

He wondered what manner of spirit this was. When he was a child he had watched as some of the tribes danced the ghost dance. He remembered stories of the great warrior spirits who would be beckoned forth to drive the white man from the lands.

He was certain that this spirit was not only aware of him, but at times encouraged him: "*follow, we will devour all*". Not ghost warriors, but the spirit of a great wolf had come to rend the white man, and Little Owl had been chosen, the only one granted the vision to see.

Throughout the day, he dozed and dreamed. Dreams of blood and glory. Startled, he would awake, afraid that it had moved on… but—no it was there. He could feel it now.

The sun had reached its apex, and soon would pass over the mountain to the west, leaving this slope in shade. He wondered if it would soon emerge. Was it a nocturnal spirit? It mattered not. When it left its den, he would again follow it.

To the south, to the homesteads and towns the white men had built. There he would join in the slaughter. Little Owl turned his face up to the sun overhead and smiled.

Chapter 18

Arthur

Big Horn Mountains, Wyoming

As we left Ten Sleep behind, I gazed surreptitiously around for any of John's "scouts". I worried that he might have them follow us to aid him in achieving this secret purpose of his. I saw no sign of any uninvited escort. Though it was unlikely that I would. I didn't know this area and they could easily find other paths that would hide them from my view.

Moo'soone was skilled and had hunted these mountains, I had to hope that he would find a way to alert me should we have company. Asking John directly would reveal our little conspiracy, so I had to hope for the best.

We followed the well-marked trail that led up into the mountains. John seemed to have some familiarity with the area and fell to speaking quietly to himself. Moo'soone was content to remain silent, all of his attention on the surrounding forest. John had said that his scouts had seen signs that the thing we sought was headed south along the range and that this trail should cut across its path.

A small herd of young deer crossed the trail ahead of us, briefly causing me to startle. I overcame it quickly and looked to my companions, who hadn't so much as flinched. I had grown lost in thought and hadn't seen them until they had come out of the undergrowth. This led me to wonder just exactly how we planned to intercept the thing—or would it also come upon us unawares?

The trail had started on an eastward tack but changed its trajectory to the north as it followed the slowly narrowing valley. We were soon surrounded by trees and further up, steep jutting arétes. From my vantage point I could now fully appreciate the incredible height of the peaks. They made our little mountain at home seem small by comparison...

Had I been on foot the sudden realization might have caused me to stumble, such was its impact. Whether from ignorance, or the inability of my mind to accept the horror, I had assumed that the events in Casper were due to some bizarre fluke of nature, a once in a millennia occurrence that would never be repeated.

And yet, Benjamin had believed that he knew what manner of thing we had faced. Meaning that there might be others. Other monstrosities, perhaps even worse than that which we had encountered. And why shouldn't such things make their home in larger, more remote mountains?

John and Moo'soone had both stopped up ahead. One looking back at me in impatience and the other with concern. I waved them on, and spurred Herodotus to catch up. I could not fall prey to unfounded fears and worries.

I resolved that should I make it off this mountain alive, I would have many questions for Benjamin. Forewarned is forearmed and there was entirely too little forewarning from my old friend.

Chapter 19

Benjamin

Salem, Massachusetts

After my return from Danvers, I left the coach behind at the house and, after declining Thomas' offer of a body-guard, began to make my way to the East India Marine Hall. I needed the walk; both to clear my head and to try and make sense of what I had learned.

Upon my arrival, I made my way to the rear of the building and was soon sitting at the small desk which had been set aside for my use for some years now. A discarded copy of the New York Journal, with its garish lead of "Congress Declares War", was currently the only occupant of the desk top. Perhaps the overly large characters were Mr. Hearst's way of celebrating our current hostilities with Spain.

It seemed that over these last few months I had somehow misplaced my formerly sanguine spirits. I looked around at the crates, with their customs stamps attesting to travel from many a far-off land and found no wonder there. My dark spirits fatigued me, and I decided to rest my head on the papery surface of the desk for just a moment…

Smell was the first of my senses to return as I awoke from a black and numbing sleep. A mixture of sea salt and a ghastly, stale, almost funginous scent greeted me. I was laying on wet sand, strangely warm liquid washing against me in small waves. The fluid caused my hearing to pop in and out as it lapped against my ears. Each time they unmuted, a strange melodious chanting reached me, and with it, a not unfamiliar series of hoots and croaks.

I felt a sudden panic as I struggled against a gluey adhesion which held my eyelids firmly shut. It was with some relief that I finally opened them to behold a caliginous sky, shot through with bands of a luminescent verdancy. I struggled to sit up, my body responding to the impetus with some delay. Now sat upright, I looked out over the strange seas before me.

There was an oddness about the way the waters flowed, they held colours murky and strange where they reflected the sky. No landmark was to be seen, adding to my sense of disconcertment. Slowly turning, I saw that the ground sloped upwards behind me, the sand continuing for a short way before the landscape became littered with huge stones.

I staggered to my feet, fighting against the wave of vertigo that assailed me and looked up at the scattered monoliths of this littoral. I saw that the sounds I had heard were made up by figures which danced and swayed in the dim light. They were familiar, and yet different: there was no sign of humanity here. I was grateful that they all faced away from me. Whatever it was that drew their attention was blocked from my sight by the mass of rock.

No boat was drawn up on this shore, no path could be seen around the gibbering mass of things which clung to or sat upon the cragged earth. The creatures became even more excited, and at the same time I felt the earth move beneath me. An earthquake surely? And yet the movement of the earth continued and grew in intensity.

The earlier sounds now became a cacophony of shrieking and madness and I clasped my hands over my ears and dropped to my knees as the earth shook so hard that I thought all must drop into the sea. The dim light grew darker, and I looked up to see what caused the change. Madness… Such a thing could not exist, this etenish thing that blotted out the sky. My screams joined the discord and I fell forward, burying my face in the sand to hide from the insanity of it…

I jumped, with heart racing, as a hand gently shook my shoulder awakening me from the horrors of my dream. The paper, now soaked through with my sweat, had adhered to the top of the small desk.

"Mr. Hathorne, are you alright?"

I turned to see Mrs. Aberg, one of the curators, looking down with a look of concern.

"Should I fetch a doctor?"

I patted her small hand where it lay on my shoulder to assure her that I was quite well. "Thank you for your concern. It was just a bad dream, nothing more. Now thank you Mrs. Aberg, please don't let me keep you from your work."

She gave me an appraising glance and, apparently satisfied, turned away and headed for the main hall. I drew in a shuddering sigh and sat back down. After a few deep breaths, I felt altogether back in the tangible world. These dreams were recurring more and more often. I could dismiss them as the byproduct of the stresses of recent days, if it wasn't for the vividness and sheer lunacy of such imaginings.

It was then that I recalled that my planned conversation with Oliver had been interrupted by my researches and it was well past time we spoke.

**

It was midday when I strode up the path home, waving in passing to a few of the men whom Thomas had hired. In spite of their rough appearance, they seemed well disciplined and capable.

Entering the vestibule, I removed my cloak and saw Oliver oiling his shotgun in the main parlor. "Where's Thomas?"

He paused with his rag in mid-stroke. "Upstairs sleeping, I believe sir. He asked for the watch this evening."

I took a seat on the edge of a Chippendale divan that sat perpendicular to the chair he had taken. Seeing that I intended on conversation, he set the shotgun down carefully. "Oliver, we cannot delay our talk any longer. I have questions for you and given our current situation, I believe only truthful answers will serve."

He looked down for a moment and when he raised his head it was as if I was looking at a different man. The veneer he had worn all these years had gone and had left a grim visage in its wake.

"Benjamin. You have to understand that I swore to your parents that I would never involve you in their affairs." He stood and motioned for me to do the same. "In spite of my efforts, you've somehow found yourself unwittingly following their very same path."

He began walking towards the western hallway, and soon we were passing through the garden room and out into the warm sunlight. I said nothing as we walked, this change in him had been unexpected. I hadn't seen emotion from him since my parents' death and it seemed to have been just as long that he had called me by my first name.

We reached the greenhouse and Oliver opened the door for me. His manners still extant, even if his servile demeanor had vanished for the moment. I breathed in the heavy scents as he took a careful look outside. He seemed satisfied that we were unobserved, and after locking the door, took the lead towards the rear of the small building.

In the rear on the ground was a porcelain pool on which floated various plants which I could not name but seemed happy with their soilless lot. It was perhaps 3 feet across, with a brick surround which held plants in various pots giving the whole space an artistically natural feel.

"Watch." Oliver knelt, and reached under some of the

foliage to release a steel latch from its cleverly hidden catch. He repeated this four times, moving clockwise around the base of the pool. Once done he was able to push against the entire contraption, causing it to slide fairly easily along the ground, until it exposed a recessed wooden hatch in the floor. It was sealed with a heavy padlock, the dark metal of it glinted with silver etchings even along the shackle.

Oliver reached behind his neck, and from within his shirt he pulled a thin chain out and over his head, from which hung a dark metal key which contained similar delicate etchings to the padlock.

He held it out to me. "In giving this to you, I have failed to keep my oath to the dead. I can only hope that what you find is of greater help than harm. Your inheritance Benjamin Hathorne."

Chapter 20
Little Owl

Big Horn Mountains, Wyoming

It was nearing dusk when Little Owl heard the scrabbling of rock coming from the crevice. He scrambled down the slope and hid amongst the trees. He did not yet know what rules might govern such a spirit. He would learn, but for now would keep his distance.

It soon crawled out and onto the surface. Paws, or were they hands? No—claws. Protuberances which seethed in constant motion making Little Owl feel nauseous. He looked down until it passed. Did the tales speak of not looking at certain spirits directly? He couldn't remember, his thoughts hazy. He would watch from the corner of his eyes; it would be made easier once on the move and following at a distance.

It was a few long minutes before it began to move. Once again it moved with unnerving speed, given its strange form of locomotion. A low groan escaped from Little Owl as he ran hard to keep up. His muscles ached from the previous night, and he feared that no amount of determination might be enough to overcome his weariness. He pushed the thought aside and focused on keeping pace.

Again, it seemed unconcerned by his presence. It began following the descending spine of the mountain, heading south as he knew it would. The rocky surface gave way to forest, which quickly grew dense. Little Owl had to slow, and risk moving from his parallel track to one that followed the great beast directly.

It was unbelievably strong and adroit, going around larger obstructions and simply plowing through the smaller ones. This left a trail that even a white man could follow in the dark. Little Owl now caught the scent left in its wake, offal mixed with something he couldn't put a name or memory to.

He reached his physical limit, and then passed it. The great wolf spirit urged him on to greater and greater feats of stamina. It would lead him to the slaughter this night. Of this he was certain.

Chapter 21

Arthur

Big Horn Mountains, Wyoming

It was nearly dusk when I began to see the hints of steel gray peeking through the foliage. We rode up another rise and a small lake fully revealed itself. It was beautifully placid in the strangely still air. It's a rare day that doesn't have even a slight breeze in Wyoming. If I believed in omens, this was surely the worst of signs.

John halted, and as I rode alongside, he pointed toward the lake's eastern shore, his face showing an intense frustration. "The trail turns east there."

"What's wrong?" I asked.

"We now have a poor choice. Find a spot along the lake to camp before night falls or continue to ride in the dark. In either case we may miss our chance."

I looked over at Moo'soone and saw that he was scanning the landscape. I had no doubt that he had both overheard and understood us. I thumbed in his direction, "What does Moo'soone think?"

John dismissed him without a look. "It is of no importance."

I held back a retort. Better if John remained ignorant of our recent partnership, however tentative. The truth was, that along the way I had started to feel a responsibility towards the young man. I felt for his loss and could understand his isolation and guilt.

I looked out over the lake in the direction of the eastern shore and then past it. From this vantage point I could not see if there was a suitable spot that would give us a wide view of the approaches should we choose to camp. "I think we should ride for the eastern shore while there is light. See what we see."

John seemed to pick up a little encouragement. "Yes. Let's see what we see."

The lake was maybe a mile across. Perhaps more in spots, the land followed its own geometry. It made for a short ride to the far shore. Once there, we had to ride a couple hundred yards more to find where the trail began to once again follow the natural gap to the east.

We hadn't seen any traffic at all during our ride, and I had seen no sign of any watchers. There had only been the same mundane wildlife we had encountered most of the way; squirrels chattering away noisily at our intrusion, rabbits hurrying into the brush, and game birds startled into flight. I found this to be a good sign, as we were likely the only ones in the immediate area.

Now that we faced yet another decision John seemed

again to be agitated and had dismounted to walk up the trail. Moo'soone gave me a look that seemed to imply contempt for the man. John may have held weight as a man of great knowledge, but even I could see that he was quickly losing the gravitas that he had held onto since our first meeting.

Moo'soone knew these mountains and was clearly very skilled at tracking, and yet here was John refusing his help. Was it distrust, or the need to prove his authority?

A sudden motion from Moo'soone caught my attention. He was looking at John, where he had stopped some 20 yards up the trail. He was no longer searching the ground but was instead holding up a small object and chanting quietly as he made a slow half turn.

Only a syllable here and there made its way back to my hearing, but I was unable make out the language regardless. It seemed that he had fallen back on whatever magicks he believed that he possessed.

I little believed in such things, even before Inkton's demise. I had no idea what difference there might be between native medicine and what Benjamin had done, which seemed semi-scientific in nature, insofar as I had seen. What I did know was that there were horrors against which such simple gestures couldn't help but seem completely inadequate.

John put his talisman back in his bag and walked back to us. "We'll camp along the lake. It is our best chance."

Moo'soone and I turned our horses and soon found a suitable spot for camp. It was far enough from the trail to be hidden from casual view, but not so close to the lake that we could end up backed into a watery corner. John hitched his horse across the campsite from ours and busied himself with his belongings.

Moo'soone pointed two fingers first at me and then towards John. The message was clear. "Watch him."

Chapter 21

Benjamin

Salem, Massachussetts

My hand shook as I carefully turned the key in the lock. Oliver stood by impassively. The lock opened with only a little resistance. It hadn't rusted, but the mechanism had clearly not seen use since my parents' deaths. Pulling the open padlock free I set it carefully to the side. I didn't know what magicks were involved in its making, but assumed they weren't meant for me.

A puff of dust greeted me upon opening the hatch. Oliver turned and fetched an oil lamp where it hung from a hook against the back wall. He lit it using a taper he had produced from some hidden place and handed it to me. "Sir, if you could carry this as you make your way down. I'll follow once you've reached the bottom. Be careful on the ladder."

I nodded, uncertain of my voice since the start of this revelation. I could feel the rust on the iron ladder rungs, and some flaked on my passing adding to the dust and forcing me to suppress a sneeze. I descended for about 20 feet, and then my leading foot felt earth beneath me. I took a step back and held the lantern high so that Oliver could follow.

I glanced around but could see little in the small cone of light emitted by the lantern. What I could see was that the ground where I stood was likely bedrock that must have been unearthed from under the alluvial soil which had once lain here.

Oliver quickly descended and once beside me held out his hand for the lantern. "If you would sir? I will need to light the other lanterns so that you can explore freely."

I handed it over and watched as his silhouetted figure walked down the short passageway that led from the hole where we had entered. It ran for perhaps 5 or 6 feet, and I followed behind him, feeling the coarse stone wall along the way. When it abruptly ended, I stopped and watched as he went forward and began to move from lantern to lantern, lighting each one. Soon I could begin to make out dark shapes amidst the amber glow and shadows thrown by the lamplight.

In the inferior light, I could see that we were in a roughly square space. It stretched open for 20 yards in each direction. The walls weren't uniform, and some had cavities that I could only associate with the charnier galleries I had seen underground in Paris. Luckily, the niches that were visible from where I stood merely contained shelving. Each holding scores of books.

The entranceway where I stood brightened as Oliver came towards me with the oil lamp, and then darkened again as he lifted the chimney and blew out the flame.

"It's best to save the oil since there is little fuel remaining in the lamps down here."

I ran my hand over the rough stone. "Did they have this constructed?"

"I never thought to ask, but I was under the impression that it had been here for some years before your parents discovered it." There was a moment of awkward silence. "Would you like to explore sir? I will then do my best to answer whatever questions you may have of me.

Without reply I began to wander. I ran my hand across the top of a dusty table, one of a number that filled the center of the room. The layout reminding me of a library. As I got closer to one of the surrounding walls, I could see that the flat areas had been filled with bookshelves and portraits. These had been decorated to the same tastes as the house. Missing from the house were the many archaic weapons hung from the stone walls or displayed in glass cases. In one corner sat what might have been a lab; modern scientific instruments were mixed with alembics and crucibles that would have suited a medieval alchemist.

Then there were the books; a strangely diverse selection from what I could make out. Ancient texts with illegible characters on worn spines were bookended by more recent works by Nietzsche and Freud. I saw at least one musical score. Such a treasure trove and collecting dust here all this time!

It was difficult to picture my parents as I remembered them in this dim place. They always seemed to be in the light; laughing and happy in my memories of them.

I turned to see that Oliver had taken a seat at one of the tables. He ran a finger across the surface and stared at it critically. "Everything is covered with so much dust."

"When did they seal it and why? And why did you not tell me?!" I rushed towards him, my hands now trembling fists. "All these years!" At this he looked up at me, and the look of desolation on his face was almost enough to counter my hurt.

"Sir. Your parents…" He trailed off and then with a short cough, resumed. "It was some months before their deaths. They had made a trip abroad. Shortly thereafter they returned and were in a great state of agitation. They sealed this place, and it was then that I was made to swear to never open it or reveal its location to anyone."

Drained of my anger, I sat down heavily in one of the chairs.

Oliver's shoulders drooped, and he looked bereft of all spirit. "I should never have broken an oath to your parents, had it not been for this threat to your life. In spite of what they may have wished, you have somehow unwittingly followed in their footsteps."

I gazed around the room and laughed bitterly. "This could have saved me years of labor."

"Sir, it was only recently that I was made aware of the danger to your person. You were careful to keep the nature of your studies to yourself."

At this I laughed with genuine mirth. "I'm sorry Oliver. You are correct and I have put you in a dreadful position. Let us make this agreement: to begin anew. I will be sure to include you in the details of my activities, to the extent that you care to be involved. And I, in turn, would welcome your expertise on any matters that touch on the same."

I held out my hand, "Agreed?"

He reached out and clasped it. "Of course sir. Gladly."

I thought about how to frame my next words. "I've often had dreams about the day they died. They've become less frequent over the years. Since last year, I've begun to have dreams of an even more disturbing nature. They contain things and places that defy description.

"Then, after all this time, I had the original dream again. Only this time…my father fought the things off fiercely and with skill. He was even effective in driving them back for a moment, as though he had experience with such matters. And…"

"And sir?"

"And then he nodded at me and struck out at me with the oar to send me overboard."

I stood up and began to pace, the sharing of such private matters causing me great discomfiture. "I have spent all these years believing that in my cowardice I failed to aid them and was struck by accident in the melee. Now, after spending my life trying to make up for my failure—I have this dream. Or memory? I no longer know which was the real version of events, and I fear that my subconscious has painted a scenario in which I don't need to feel guilt."

Oliver mulled this over for a minute. "It sounds like your father as I remember him. He knew his fate and he loved you and your sister more than anything. He would have taken any risk to save your life. After they sealed this place, there was always a wariness about them. You may not remember, but they became extremely vigilant when it came to you and your sister's safety."

I stopped treading my semi-circular path between desks. "The dream was the most vivid and clear that it has ever been. It also seemed to me that the look he gave me conveyed that the attack hadn't been entirely unexpected and that he had been prepared to fight to his death." I gestured at the room in general. "It seems now that he did have something to share with me after all."

I sighed as I took in the contents of the room. I would have to catalogue it all, and compare their researches with my own. All of which would have to wait. Still, I wanted to spend a little more time here, where my parents had worked together. "Oliver, would you mind checking on our Hessians? If they've begun to eat the fine china, I will be quite cross. I will join you shortly."

"Of course sir. Take your time." His departing footsteps were quiet as he crossed the rough stone with its thin overlay of fine dirt.

I sat back at the desk and picked up a dusty journal. Upon opening it to the first page I saw the date and a brief summary of the topic written in my father's crablike handwriting, so similar to my own. A source of irritation to my mother.

It appeared that he had also created a series of short codes to organize the volumes, and by my reasoning there was likely dozens of such journals, if not more.

I picked up another at random, and idly flipped through the pages, knowing that I could dive into them with much greater attention once things had settled. I passed another of my mother's carefully depicted images, penciled on one of the final pages. I had begun to lay the journal down with the others, when a sudden recollection caused me to open it again. I leafed back some three or four pages until I saw what had caught my attention.

It was a ghastly and abhorrent thing, drawn with meticulous detail by my mother's deft hand. An image both horrible and familiar. It resembled the crudely carved statuette that had, until recently, adorned my desk. Under the drawing, a name by which I could now refer to it: *Cthulhu*.

Chapter 22

Arthur

Big Horn Mountains, Wyoming

I was wakened by a sharp jab in the ribs. A tired looking John looked down at me where I lay bleary-eyed in my bedroll. "Your watch. I have seen nothing." There was disappointment in his voice. "Make sure you wake me immediately if anything approaches." He tossed his improvised waking stick into the brush and headed towards his bedroll.

I got up slowly, with only a few stifled groans and walked away from the embers of our earlier fire. John had insisted that we only use it for our supper and then let it burn out. It was clear that John had tried and failed to extend his watch throughout the entire night.

I looked over to where Moo'soone lay and could see the shine of his eyes staring back. I guessed that he hadn't slept at all. I waved and made a series of hand signals meant to convey that I would wake him first should I see anything during my watch. He gave no indication of understanding, so either my attempts at communicating looked like visual gibberish, or he simply refused to sleep. I shrugged and went in search of a tree to put my back against, one that would give me a good view of both the trail and the surrounding woods.

I glanced back and could see the moon painting a line of light across the lake and thought about how nice a bath would feel. With all the rush I hadn't even thought to look for a wash basin while we were in Ten Sleep. My face was itchy after these few days without seeing a razor. I had decided against packing it, it having been a gift from Catherine and therefore irreplaceable.

It was the nights when I missed her most. Lying in my bedroll, with just cold empty ground where her presence would have otherwise warmed me. How quickly a man's way of life changes. The light across the water changed, and I looked up to see where the moon and a few visible stars shone from an opening in the clouds creating a sort of celestial glade.

I was pulled from my reverie by the far-off scream of an animal. I immediately crouched and rested a hand on my revolver as I listened carefully to see if it was repeated. The high walls of the canyon caused the sound to echo and disperse in a way that made it difficult to judge the distance.

I felt a hand softly grasp my shoulder, as Moo'soone crouched next to me, having moved silently alongside with his bow strung and arrow nocked. He whispered, "Not close, not far."

We remained in that position for several minutes, when the quiet was disturbed by a brief yelp. It echoed through the dark canyon and this time I was certain it had been much closer. Moo'soone made a sound like a curse and hissed. "Fast!"

Now I could hear furtive sounds behind me and turned to see John rifling quickly through one of his bags. Having gathered together what he sought after, he walked in a crouch over to our position. One of his bags slung over his left shoulder. In his right hand he gripped together what looked like an engraved stave and the small object that he had used earlier in the day.

"Why didn't you wake me?!" He said, in an angry sotto voce. He touched on the arrow that Moo'soone had nocked, forcing the bow downwards.

"It could be any manner of animals hunting at night." I whispered back angrily, though I knew this to be a lie.

He stared into the gloom for a moment. Then stood fully upright and walked a short distance onto the trail and centered himself there. He again began to chant in the strange tongue that I had only caught a few morphemes of earlier. It was a harsh language and stirred a disquiet in me.

Moo'soone had left my side while I had been watching this display, his return almost unnoticed so quickly had he moved. I noticed that he now carried his spear as well. There was a grim look on his face, but his hand did not tremble.

He pulled at my arm and we both moved forward, to take up more defensive positions near John. I on his left and Moo'soone to his right.

John had removed the bag at his neck and shook a powder out of it which he then blew into the air after a particularly emphatic chant. It shimmered in the moonlit night and slowly fell to the ground. He did not stop in his incantation or evocation, instead he held aloft the stave in one hand and the talisman in the other and continued on even more loudly.

I had no idea what he was attempting to achieve, nor did I very much care. I now felt that melding of fear and despair that tickled my spine with its familiarity. That I could not hear the sounds of the forest over John's incomprehensible recitation made it even worse. I drew my right revolver and looked to where Moo'soone stood looking straight into the forest. He was focused on a space in front of John and just to his left.

I focused my vision there, knowing that he had the keener senses. In just a matter of seconds I could hear something crashing through the trees and brush. It was something large. Even John paused, and in that silence the strange arrhythmic tread of the thing became even louder.

It emerged from the tree-covered hillside and onto the trail, not far from where John stood. And in spite of my experiences, I stood momentarily awestruck.

The outline of a wolf-like shape. Enveloped with ropy sinuous protuberances alive with that same alien movement that I had seen devour friends and neighbors. Ghastly shapes that shifted in and out of its greater form, sometimes coalescing into almost human semblances. What might have served as its face was now just a jumbled collection of needle-like fangs circling a gaping maw of human-looking molars. Its sole monstrous orbit was filled with a wet and suppurating yellow eye. The entirety of the thing was splattered with blood and offal and gave off a nauseating stench.

It had slowed to pace some 10 feet from John, who stared at it aghast and was now, finally, stunned into silence. I thumbed back a hammer and aimed my right revolver directly at that yellow orb. Without hesitation, I pulled the trigger…which fell with a faint click on a cartridge which failed to fire. My stomach dropped. With the speed of long practice, I drew my left revolver while thumbing the next cartridge into place—and heard the thrum of a bowstring.

An arrow now sprouted from the creature's side, but it made no sound. It moved with alien grace to turn its sickly amber orb on Moo'soone who was charging it, with his spear in hand, letting out a roar that was part war cry and part scream of rage and anguish. He leapt into the air, throwing his spear at the flank of the thing, and then he twisted in the air, metal flashing incongruously from his back as I heard another cry, this time one of pure maddened rage. "NOOO!"

A young, unfamiliar Indian had emerged from the trees and was running towards where Moo'soone had landed. I fired with my right hand in reflex and saw his body jerk once, and again as the second round also found its mark. He slid to a stop amidst a floor of pine needles.

In the single instant this had all transpired, I found that the thing had moved past John and was moving with startling speed towards me. I could see Moo'soone's spear deep in its side, the shaft waving along with the strange movements.

I raised both revolvers to fire, when the right one was knocked painfully from my hand. John had hammered at it with the small stone that he had been using in his medicine just seconds ago. "No. You mustn't," he breathed heavily, "It's our god."

Even as the last word passed his lips, I fired every round in my left Colt, and saw each of them strike true, directly in the center of that mass of deadly sharp spines. The thing let out an unearthly sound, discordant with overtones and with enough volume to drop me to my knees. I covered my face, but still the light crackled and spit and pierced through me. That familiar eldritch light, but on a scale that lit the canyon and, even as it faded, left a dusting of strangely colored motes to slowly disappear into the ground.

I was shaking but determined to stand and make my way over to check on Moo'soone, uncertain of what I'd seen in those few chaotic moments but fearing the worst. A strong hand clamped down on my shoulder, stopping my weak upward momentum. I knew it was John, but we'd have time later to work out any discord, I needed to see to Moo'soone.

I felt a sharp pain under my left ear, followed by a wave of internal heat, and then the woods and Moo'soone's limp body all began to swim in my vision. A hand cupped my jaw tightly, preventing me from falling face forward. Motes of white began to creep around the edges of my vision as I tried to cling to consciousness.

John's face was suddenly inches from my own. His visage was filled with such a hate that he appeared like a demon to my poisoned senses. He said nothing, simply stared until the white became everything and I knew no more.

May 1898

Epilogue

Big Horn Mountains, Wyoming

We ascended the flattened summit with the warming day left behind us, now replaced with a biting chill. It wasn't just the wind, there was a sense of something deeply wrong here. I studied the geometrically placed stones and wondered at their purpose. I had seen drawings of other such constructs created by native peoples the world over.

Our guide knelt at the edge, and pointed towards the center, seemingly unwilling to enter the circle proper. I dismounted and walked carefully in the direction he pointed. I was loathe to disturb the ground; aware of the importance it held to the native peoples here, and needing to preserve any signs that our tracker might decipher.

As I grew closer, I saw the splattering of rust coloring the rocks. My heart sunk. More blood. But why here?

I stood. Slowly looking around the summit, my gaze caught the sight of Catherine from where she sat under the carriage hood. Even in the poor light of dusk, her wan complexion was visible and her ice blue eyes seemed to burn with an inner light. I continued my survey as I waited for our guide to try and find another trail. I was exhausted and ached from the journey, but neither I, nor Catherine, would give up this search.

I had received Catherine's letter in Salem in response to the parcel and note I had sent to Arthur. When she explained where Arthur had gone and why, I dropped everything and boarded the soonest available train. I left Oliver with instructions to continue to run the household and spoke in detail with Thomas about maintaining security in my absence. Given recent revelations, I now suspected that I was no longer in danger of another direct attack. It was another long week before I arrived again in Casper.

I could not help but blame myself for Arthur's predicament; I could not think of it as a loss, not yet. When he had asked for my help, I had shared with him just enough knowledge to make it impossible to assuage his guilt should the threat return.

As I looked around the circle of stones, something caught my eye. A shape that did not mesh with the natural geometry of the area. I moved forward to the whitened center stone and found the object. A statuette. One that, not long ago, had been a simple ornament to my desk in Salem. No clearer message was needed.

I walked slowly back to the carriage, not knowing what I might say to Catherine but preparing myself for the long ride to come.

***

It was dusk when I finally opened the door to my meagre room. One of the two that we had managed to acquire in Buffalo. My valise had grown heavy, and I simply wanted to retire to my bed. However, the day's events kept replaying in my mind; a continuous loop that fueled a cycle of frustration, fear and anger. The room was dim, as the last of the sunlight filtered through slightly tattered curtains.

I let out a slight groan as I bent and set my bag down just inside the door. I slowly rose, my hands pressing at my aching lower back when I caught a distinctly feminine scent and stiffened. I started to reach toward the gun at my hip when a lightly accented voice said softly, "Hello Benjamin."

The voice came from the settee in the corner of the sparsely furnished room, and I took slow steps forward until I could make out the dark shape that sat there. Her alabaster face seemed to almost luminesce, framed as it was by raven hair in the gloaming. In the same moment, I caught the glint of the small pistol which she had pointed at me. I sighed.

"Hello Bella."

Acknowledgements

I would like to thank my parents for encouraging me to keep writing, even during dark times. My dog Skippy for keeping my feet warm, no matter where I choose to sit. Thanks to Badger Editing Services for the proof reading. And no, that paragraph didn't make any sense. Finally, to my readers: I hope you enjoy this long overdue second volume, and find in it, some reward for your patience. If this should be your first-time meeting Arthur and Benjamin; thank you for reading and welcome.

About the Author

Max Beaven resides in Northwest Montana, where he walks the forests with his dog Skippy. He has yet to see a wendigo.

Follow the author at: https://www.maxbeaven.com